The Rhymer

an Heredyssey

"The oldest and best stories in the world were told rhythmically, lyrically, with the music of beauty, terror, loss and longing. It's a form that has fallen somewhat into disuse in recent decades, and that's a shame. But Douglas Thompson, a new writer of immense promise, is helping to find this wondrous method again, to ensure that the newest and best stories are also told rhythmically, lyrically, with the music of beauty, terror, loss and longing, and, in *The Rhymer*, to additionally fuse the form with modern and unique concepts, to create an effect that is richly complex but simply stupendous."

– Rhys Hughes, writer and essayist

"Obviously Thompson is a risk-taker, a dare-devil member of the literati, to propose such a feat as [*The Rhymer*]... But Thompson's risks are calculated. He is a master craftsman, pulling out all the stops with exceptional timing (comic and otherwise)."

– Rachel Kendall, writer and editor of *Sein und Werden*
(from the introduction)

On Douglas's earlier books:

"Thompson has certainly shown he is a name to watch."

– Ian Sales, *Interzone* Magazine

"Thompson writes with the assurance of someone completely in control of his material, bringing the story alive on the page."

– Peter Tennant, *Black Static* Magazine

The Rhymer

an Heredyssey

Douglas Thompson

Elsewhen Press

The Rhymer, an Heredyssey
First published in Great Britain by Elsewhen Press, 2014
An imprint of Alnpete Limited

Elsewhen Press, PO Box 757, Dartford, Kent DA2 7TQ
www.elsewhen.press

British Library Cataloguing in Publication Data.
A catalogue record for this book is available from the British Library.
ISBN 978-1-908168-41-2 Print edition
ISBN 978-1-908168-51-1 eBook edition

Designed and formatted by Elsewhen Press

Contents

For Rachel Kendall

In memory of Joel Lane (1963-2013)
the greatest of all of us.

Introduction

by Rachel Kendall

When Douglas Thompson submitted the first part of The Rhymer (titled Heredyssey) to *Sein und Werden* it made me feel a little bit giddy. I'd published his work in previous issues and was a big fan of this self-labelled Glasgow-surrealist but here was a story unlike anything I had read before. In the best possible way. Here was an excerpt, workable as a stand-alone piece, written almost entirely in verse. Obviously Thompson is a risk-taker, a dare-devil member of the literati, to propose such a feat as this. Should the measurements be out of sync, the angles a bit skewed or the trajectory off course, this could have been disastrous. But Thompson's risks are calculated. He is a master craftsman, pulling out all the stops with exceptional timing (comic and otherwise).

When I accepted Heredyssey I told Thompson I would love to read a full-length novel written in the same poetic style. I knew Heredyssey was already a longer piece but when Thompson told me there was a whole novel in the pipeline I was thrilled. Barely a couple of months down the line, Heredyssey, now titled The Rhymer, appeared in my inbox.

Let me just say, at this point, that Thompson works part-time as an architect (and full-time as a writer if his literary output is anything to go by). This is not something I'm mentioning in passing. To me, architecture is one of those mysterious schools that straddles both science and art, one that demands artistic freedom within the constraints of mathematical equation. Taking much of his influence from the whorls and fronds of nature, the architect can create in months what nature took a billion years or just a few seconds to develop. But whether he is inspired by the crystal or the snowflake the architect must be a methodical, patient perfectionist with a healthy mix of left and right brain activity, someone who can work on the delicate minutiae whilst keeping sight of the bigger picture. And these traits are not limited to Thompson's day job. I believe he builds his stories in much the same way he plans his physical structures. To Thompson every word, every sentence is significant. He is one of those authors for whom writing is more than just the telling of a good story. It is a finely honed craft. This is true of all his work, not just The Rhymer. Take, for instance, his short story *My (Ruined) Father*, an immaculately constructed piece of prose that juxtaposes the slow disintegration of a building with the deteriorating health of the narrator's father.

> *'I have seen the old photos. My father had a fine face (façade) once, a good (bone) structure, captivating pair of big eyes (windows), and a strong dignified looking mouth (shopfront).'*

Evocative, tender and visual, Thompson's writing creates feeling in everything, be it natural or man-made. Similarly in *The Fallen Woman* he creates emotion and intuition in physical constructs, merging the sentient with the composite and turning solid into fluid.

> *'Look: a falling figure hits the water and half the world collapses inwards. Lurching of heart and lungs. Towerblocks double-over in pain, bridges spin round in half-recognition.'*

Just as Duchamp's Woman Descending a Staircase was an attempt to portray movement and altered perspectives, Thompson uses rhetoric to expose every point of view, every narrative and every context until characters begin to converge in bas-relief. Because emotions are never just black or white, and personality is not a linear composition, Thompson's characters are complex and intricate with changing attitudes and inconsistent behaviours. In what may almost be called a study of form, another work by the author – Sylvow – begins with a man taking several photographs of a flower, from every conceivable angle, only to discover that *'every flower and leaf has turned itself towards him'*. In Thompson's world nothing adheres to the laws of physics, solid floors liquefy, human-machine hybrids emerge and reality and memory distort and converge, and like Escher's unfathomable stairs and Dali's melting clocks, The Rhymer is a visual mind-bender, a puzzle to be solved.

But Thompson never insults his readers' intelligence by giving the game away. He does drop a few screwy clues here and there and plants some cock-eyed signs to lead us on our merry way, but never does he give us more than he wants to. The fun is in solving the mystery ourselves after all and The Rhymer is a mystery, albeit an existential one. Who is this man, this philosopher-poet who seems to have lost his memory of time and place? Is he a seer? A mad man? He is searching, but for what exactly? Is it love that drives him on? Or the question of self? Or the even bigger question of God? Like a character in a computer game he must find the clues along with us, gaining points with every correct answer and to reach the highest level is to reach enlightenment is to discover who he actually is.

But is enlightenment reached through affirmation or denial? Is the personality established through a process of building up or cutting down? The Rhymer's characters wear masks, hide their features and change their appearance in true dream-like form, but do they do so in order to cast doubt or to raise questions? These characters are more than just members of the chorus; they're part of the vehicle transporting Nadith (let me refer to him thus, to avoid confusion) through time, space and sur-reality.

'This mask thing is a metaphor of course, but then again it isn't. I really am a new person every time, made instantly into what the first of my lost audience yearn for. In that sense, this polished metal face is a mirror,

dragging everything in from around it, and by the very contours of its features: fluidly distorting.'

Nadith, then, isn't just a seer; he's also a truth-teller. He is the reflection of society's whims, mankind's mistakes. He empathises, but he doesn't attempt to cross any bridges. He teaches through disclosure, yet this is not his calling. He has fallen into the realm of sooth-sayer while all he really wants to do is find his brother and gain some insight into his past.

Zenir (let us call him) is his brother's polar opposite. While Nadith, the humble drifter, isn't always likeable, Zenir is always detestable. Vanity, greed and superficiality are just some of his vices and he is rolling in the excesses of a profitable artistic career. Because of this he always seems to be one furlong, mile or art gallery ahead. And so Nadith chases his brother's shadow through Suburbia, Industria, Oceania, Sylvia and Urbis where geography and grey matter seem to converge. We see nature encroaching on the concrete jungle in an effort to reclaim its space; we see the prophetic vision of (wo)man-made machines...

'... a carefully substantiated and cross-referenced theory with footnotes, that only dreamt it was a woman, only a pale worm left behind like a thing spilled from an anatomist's pickling jar, broken on the wheel of learning. And crucified now on the spokes of a bicycle.'

and the plight of the suburban lawn...

'And in this quiet street we walk through, how all the trees and bushes and hedgerows seem hushed and hunched over like monks in hoods immersed in green hymns, asleep in their pews, the timber fences of suburbia which keep them confined and subdued'.

...all, perhaps, sites of longing and mourning for that which Nadith seeks. As a transient, he is the leaf blown this way and that, into the onslaught of traffic, the noise and fury of the material world. He will never fit into their spaces, but that's okay because he prefers the sky as his roof and the grass as his bed. And so he drifts, from beginning to end, destined perhaps to repeat and repeat ad infinitum.

Should this book come with a warning? '... contains surreal imagery and disturbing verse. May offend.'? I don't think so. If anything, I think it could prove to be a pleasant surprise for the unsuspecting genre-reader. And it's not as though this technique has been employed just for a bit of fun. I'm sure it was fun to write, almost as much fun as it is to read, but there's more to it. Language is a hinge and verse is a lubricant. There's no easier way to teach and inform someone learning to read than by repetition and rhyme.

'Uncurling, serpent Zenir slithers through the contours of their bowels, lengthening their vowels, promoting their taste for pretension, distancing themselves from each other by claims they can lay to his vision, acquisition in material transposition of the spiritual windows he opens.'

By the time you reach the end of The Rhymer you still won't have all the answers, though you'll be surprised by those you do have. Just as this tale refuses to squeeze into any one genre, so it will baulk at fitting within your expectations. I promise you will want to go back and re-read sections, reacquaint yourselves with characters, re-imagine logistics, and still you won't know, for sure, who is what or why. And that is how it should be. There are clues to the past and there are hints at the present, but who's to say if these are dreams, reality, or the ravings of a lunatic. Read it, enjoy it, and when you've figured it out, give me a call.

Rachel Kendall, Jan 2014

PART

ONE

Suburbia

Melancholy, soliloquy. Hunger and a hundred questions burning in the heart. Turbulence of storm clouds, these tree tops raging in the forest I carry inside me. What it means to be abroad in this world and always searching. And Nature my church. I pray by walking through Her. Endlessly it seems, always trying to lose this body like the pathetic ballast it is, flopping puppet buffeted by futile gestures, the human mime. I wear a new mask for each new town I come down into, after weeks and months of pilgrimage on high plains pacing under this sun, the moon and stars. I sleep in hedgerows, haystacks, I waken with the dawn or when the snout of some curious animal intrudes, investigating my warmth and smells. If only I could learn of their conclusions, know myself, the ancient puzzle as the Greeks first phrased it.

Sometimes it begins with a church spire, like the old days, glimpsed across swaying wheat fields, tolling of bells resounding in my feet. Or more often now with distant tower blocks, hell's teeth, or some swishing by-pass, the constant cars, whizzing hot metal like buzzing flies engaged in a feeding frenzy upon the corpse of civilisation. Because this is how it always is at the end, the selfishness made manifest, the isolation devices, the rash of rush and bluster. What face shall I make for myself today, to meet such people? One forged in steel perhaps, to glimmer, to join the clamour, for valour, for glamour. Warlike music in my tongue and blood, make ready for the great reunion.

This mask thing is a metaphor of course, but then again it isn't. I really am a new person every time, made instantly into what the first of my lost audience yearn for. In that sense, this polished metal face is a mirror, dragging everything in from around it, and by the very contours of its features: fluidly distorting. And then the mask fits, clicks seamlessly into place, as do I, and no one knows the difference. Except myself who, trapped underneath and subtly starved of air over coming days and weeks, suffocates oh so slowly, until sweating, panicking, in the end breaks free and bursts out from some quaint domestic door in the early hours and embarks once more upon the world, eyes lifted, drinking the sky, as it were: the elixir of the soul. And the sun, my gold, fills my pockets, makes me rich and well again.

Today I find a dead deer by the roadside, struck by their hurtling carriages, its carcass bleeding, not long dead, still warm. But wait. I haven't told you about the contraption yet, homemade, strapped with tape to my chest, and the wires trailing down both my sleeves. I reach a hand between two buttons of my shirt to turn a dial then plug my wires into the beast's neck and replay its last hours and minutes briefly in fast forward, flash frame, flicker picture. And then after the jolt, satisfied as by a potent shot of coffee or firewater, I lift the deer onto my back and wear it like a crown, forelegs draped around my neck crisscrossed in front scarf-like, primitive costume, totem, token, atavistic, head dress of a former age, of what they've lost, the pallid insipid ones, the pride and primitivism, antique rage. Let me remind them.

I march down into their pretty country town through all the quiet carefully tended streets, past their immaculate gardens between prim hedgerows. How Nature weeps to be free, imprisoned there, enslaved in flowerbeds, chained in trellises, crucified by the cloche. And all the time sweet red blood oozes down my neck and chest from my hoisted prize. At first a few cars slow, turning, jaded eyes within, goggling. Then some gardeners gasp, retreat down dusty pathways. I stand at traffic lights in magnificent disgrace, parties of school children being paraded by in buses, white faces turned, spattered across their disbelieving screens as meadow flowers or gunfire, loosestrife. Then at last I walk into the little town centre and solemnly approach the foot of their war monument: a bronze lady on a marble pedestal, some grotesquely misunderstood and misdrawn goddess, rising from her knees to lift a burning flame of holy carnage heavenwards in thanks for wars and the blood of young men. She wants more it seems, always more, rapacious for futility. And I take down the bleeding deer and lay it at her feet.

A policeman approaches. Stout, stupid pillar of the law, his notebook bristling. I try to tell him the number plate and the face of the man who slew the deer in his speeding pedal car, a builder apt to dump his debris in rural hedgerows after a day overcharging the idle rich for unnecessary house extensions for children who never come home, but he seems to think me mad. Imagine, in a world this lunatic. I bid him lean in a little closer then I prise off my mask to give him a little glimpse of what lurks beneath and that does the trick, sends him scuttling off like a crab longing for a rock to hide under. I make my way across the cobbled precinct to the old pub, drawn by some ancient music leaking from an open door. Inside somebody passes me a fiddle and I join in, unleash a trail of notes borrowed from circling birds glimpsed on the high moors, semi-quavers gurgled from the mouth of fishes in tinkling burns. And when I'm done a pint of golden amber is placed on the table in front of me, instantly everybody's friend, no need for money. I reach up to scratch my chin and find the joint-lines are gone, the mask is fused, too late for an escape now.

A fellow takes a place beside me, a little weasel of a man, all white tousled beards and dreadlocks, skin nearly as dark as mine. *Nadith*, he calls me, so there we have it, a name. And says I have a brother, *Zenir*, who just went through here a few weeks ago, a fine and successful man, a great artist with a promising future rearing up before him like a tidal wave. He talked about me often, Weasel says, this Zenir, about his special little brother, a master of music and words as he is of colour and shape, a traveller between towns. I am that man now, am I not? And who am I to argue? He must take me to *Elissa* he says, whoever that is, who will have a message from him. But first I must have another drink of golden amber and sit in on their club. *What club? —I say. Rotary, notaries? Masonic, platonic, knitting, hair-splitting, reading, bleeding, badger baiting, masturbating?*

No, just watch he says, and it must be the nectar: he reaches out and lifts the black-and-white chequers of the floor tiles up as if he is tweaking my eyelid and the whole floor distorts with everything on it. There is a light pouring in a steady white line from beneath the far wall, and Weasel pulls on the floor like a carpet. He's drawing us closer to it as everyone else crumples and bends out of shape like sweety-papers. Soon the bright white light is in my face, at the base of the tall wall, about to slurp under and I let myself go, flowing, glowing, into the locked room beyond.

Weasel is in his element here, what a crew. The sky-gazers and weather-watchers club, who lounge around in angled chairs beneath a huge skylight, a Victorian gazebo, lantern, conservatory, orangerie, cupola, cornucopia of glass and steel all pleasantly musty and in need of a good paint, although to do so would mean stripping the old lead paint off first, inhalation of which would drive some unfortunate handyman a madman slowly until he began wetting his trousers and falling over six months later, then death. So better not bother. The fug of cigar smoke is prodigious here, we thought they'd banned it, along with freewill, predestination, self-immolation and other innocent pleasures. *So what gives? –* opines Nadith, adopting the hip vernacular to an old avuncular: Doctor Tolleson by name, who looks in charge-ish. Introductions are made and instantly forgotten as is the custom here and anywhere. A Cynthia Beiderbecker, retired occupational therapist, which sounds like a contradiction in terms or at least a non-sequitur but I desist from the jibe advisedly, watching Weasel's eyes. Secateurs, the weapon of choice of our next: Joyce, John, a gardener. Then sequesters: Henry Packer, quite a card, a banker, a gambler then with others' money, soon we'll have the whole pack: two more. A Mary Winston, with Churchill's jowls and jocularity. Bill Heaney, heinous in his choice of cardigans at least and doubtless much else still to be revealed pre-judging by the shifty face, first impressions of a difficult birth that failed to strangle him.

Our club, says Tolleson, puffing like a steam train, eyes magnified in fishbowl fright behind his glasses, *considers the notion that we are all dead, us humans, and all this that we think life now is but an afterlife. How else to account for the ridiculous preponderance of coincidence, the déjà vu, the way what books we read constantly prefigure our everyday concerns, the way the pet cat leaps up a second before the phone goes, the way I think of my Aunty Jean and then she calls me.*

Moreover, interjects Packer, so violently that I think he means move over and nearly jump from the chair myself like said prophetic feline, *–we find that sitting here and staring up at these clouds, sometimes of a languid afternoon we gain glimpses through the shifting gossamer tissues of celestial modesty and spy the true people up there naked, huge giants* *glimpsed from below at difficult angles, going about their real and proper lives of which these below are only confused memories, shadows and echoes thrown on a forest floor in which we wander lost as children.*

Well spoken, winces Mary Winston, born to be a librarian, winsome in her smiles that her closed eyes and furrowing brow constantly lose track of, as she drags huge thoughts into the light of day from her dusty cognitive attic. *You would not believe the considerable detail we have divined from here through sheer unadulterated persistence, of the lives of the Titans as it were, the huge heroic people we were each before we were woken by death and birth into this becalmed shore of suburban banality, a domain one might say of air-freshener and furniture polish, of broken dreams and haemorrhoid creams, where even semen is semi-skimmed, pasteurised and ultra-heat treated. And what do you think, Mister Nadith?* (Old Tolleson chokes on his tea at that last, as if to wish he'd had it black).

Now there's the crunch, they've got me cornered. I take my time, lighting a huge cigar that I have no intention of smoking. At last, Olympian, the flame catches. *Eternal recurrence you mean of course, I am familiar with it, the most unthinkable of Nietzsche's theories, but even it is a metaphor for the ineffable, the inedible, don't you think? So why shouldn't Buddhist reincarnation and Christian damnation and all the other tosh be rated as equal tosh with all other tosh, fragments of a jigsaw of tosh that cannot be completed or viewed by those still living? Photographs of the same weird object viewed from different angles? Indeed, might we not consider human beings as metaphors themselves, and then for what, would be the next inevitable question. I say we are all asleep, and only art can wake us up for a few mad moments each day, but if we could but catch all those moments like falling rose petals on the dark polished wood of the lid of a grand piano on a summer's day in the drawing room of a quiet house, and read them like tea leaves, then we might hold the truth quivering in our quivering hands like a captured bird, but even then to hold it long would kill it.*

Extraordinary, extraordinary, John Joyce interjects, ejaculates, ejects adroitly (Tolleson covers his tea), *-Your command of words, your insanely elliptical diction. Is there a guidebook one can purchase on you, as if you were a National Trust-entrusted castle, or a blog one can follow so devoutly nightly and daily as to lose one's job gaily, gaining one's employer's contempt and derision not to say one's P45 on a platter?*

No, alas... I sigh in faux despair, *I am just all me, and tomorrow I will be someone different.*

Back to reincarnation then, Beiderbecker mumbles, bumbles, *if indeed we ever left it.*

And leaving is what we must do next, Weasel says, rising, *I've promised to take Nadith to meet Elissa,* hoping to save me from Heaney whose eyes and ears have taken all in and whose gorge is rising to a mighty declamation.

Nadith, before you go, he stands, his waistcoat buttons popping like distant shells on the fields of Flanders, *-you must take our card and call again, we should like to have you in our club, you theorise like only the truly idle can muster, and sport the foul breath and body odour that in my experience only two categories of men ever possess: great writers and the homeless.*

Perhaps they are the same thing, I say as my parting short, pausing at the door, and farting for good measure.

*

What a jolly old time, not. But the pedestrian precinct is quelled and quieted, the crowds mostly buggered off, laying off from their shopping at last, by the time we emerge from that den of obscurantists by what route I can't remember. I am left with the impression that the room I have just exited existed not at the back of any pub, let alone that one, but at the back of any mind led so astray as to entertain it. I vow not to again. Sunset is not long off as Weasel hurries me past the brassy thighs of vainglorious Athena or Boudica, or whatever she is, the statue's pedestal still visibly stained by my late offering, but not a bone of it left, and I wonder what dog nibbled there or what butcher plundered for his choicest cuts, had he the wisdom.

Walking westwards the blood red sun is pierced by the lance of a steeple, light dribbling from the wound, snagging hazily in yellow blurring haloes around gravestones, tombs, sepulchres, lairs, grottoes and the like. And I pause for a second, sniffing dog-like, straining on the invisible leash by which Weasel seeks to drag me, tensing, to kneel and examine a few graves. Putting down roots, I sit down with my back against the wall of the auld kirk for a moment and plug my sleeve wires into the mossy stones, turning the dial on my chest like a radio set, tuning into the waves, afore and aft, astral sailor at the bridge of present time. The willows weep, the yew yawns, the ancient oaks open up their secrets. I watch a legion of Roman soldiers emerge from one wall and march across to vanish through another. I can almost smell them, the sweat and olives, the spilt blood of savages still misting their tired eyes. They will be ambushed presently, by my obliging ancestors. I could stay and go back to plunder further time for Norsemen's raids and echoing prayers of monks in rough sackcloth, glinting altar pieces, jewels and armour, but Weasel is tugging at me and we must away.

Weasel leads me through the resplendent gardens of suburbia, maze-like, parterre walls of hedge and bush, losing both of us quickly in the failing light as the orange sodium blossoms droop from overhead, strange fruit on iron trees. I am suddenly haunted by fragmented memories of childhood, coming home from school on winter evenings. So I was a child once, with a mother somewhere. But the dark window closes as quickly as it opens before I can catch sight of... What? There it is again, Weasel, walking always slightly ahead as if dragging me like a sleigh across snowfields, is jabbering again about my having a brother. The streets get quieter and posher, passover kosher, hushed in bushes, hunched in bunches of branches, carefully tended and mended, until we arrive at the door: fine iron gates in voluptuous curves and Weasel squeaking into an intercom like an over-awed overwrought urchin.

We are in, up a winding path then through large carved doors into an interior like an ornate lighthouse burning in the confused night, a temple of unreason. Then strangely, Weasel is gone, out like a rat through a tradesman's entrance, leaving me to Elissa. I feel naked, like a morsel poised upon a trap. She comes down her long hallway, a swishing of white satin, flowing and pouring, a soft storm pinned by two red lips and above them a nose which sniffs at the blood on my stained shirt. *You bear such a resemblance to him! –she shrieks, -to Zenir! Let me look at you, your profile.* She turns my cheek with hands of a practised film director or perhaps a manqué hairdresser. *The nose, the aquiline profile, that Arabic brow, or are you of Armenian, Persian descent... I forget?*

I forget also... I say, sotto voce, eyes down, aiming for modesty. Then she plunges me into her studio, her salon, to show me Zenir's pictures.

Look, Nadith, isn't it? He told me so much about you. When did you two last meet? He's always on the move. Look at these pictures. I bought far too many of course, but I simply couldn't restrain myself. He is in his prime, this is the mother lode of inspiration he's ploughing these days, have you ever seen such strangeness, such illumination?

Now at last, used as I am to trees and skies and the green and natural things that spring from the fields and seas of terrestrial creation, I must admit that these paintings make me halt, break step, break wind, skip breath, skip breakfast, jump ship, jump backwards. Each canvas is huge and hugely strange. Here one is a crab, transforming into the face of a man, then into the scene of a sea cliff, a landscape in wondrously sad light. And here is one of a flock of horses galloping through the air and turning into clouds then into the white dress of a young woman falling backwards her golden hair lifting up in strands and turning into a halo around a summer sun. And yet another of a tree of red apples but each apple is a bullet hole and the tree is also a hand, the branches and leaves the lines on the palm, and there is something inside of each bullet hole, other tiny scenes that draw me in and I'm starting to feel sick as I bend down to look closer into one, when Elissa's hand on my shoulder brings me back to my senses with a jolt.

What was it like to grow up with him? –Such a great artist, did you watch him doing his first sketches, did you play together? Did you urinate together, taking care to generate convergent streams from alternate sides of the water closet? Where does he get his ideas?

Enough! I raise my fingers to my lips, then my temple, wishing it was one. *It was a difficult childhood. We were often separated by our obstreperous governess.*

Obstreperous?

Yes, she was an obstetrician. I mean... an optician... a magician.

A musician?

That as well, certainly. A polymath.

A mathematician?

A polymathematician then, shall we settle on that?

Appallingly. Assuredly. It accounts for your extensive education.

Elissa is an exceptionally tall woman. Her head always seems to be out of focus somewhere above me, dimmed in a swirl of blonde hair haloed by her halogen lights in smoked glass lampshades. And between the paintings, I can see Art Nouveau stained-glass windows with cryptic glimpses of meadows beyond. We are on the outskirts of town now, where she has bagged herself the best views. But the interiors are old, Arts and Crafts, Jugendstil, Fin de siècle, sinuous curves and languid androgynes. *Education? I'm not sure I get your drift...* -I reply, and we do seem to be drifting, from the studio to the parlour from the parlour to the boudoir. We must get back to the Renoir. Ce Soir.

Zenir told me, how your nanny gave you your first sexual experiences.

Did he indeed? How indiscreet of him. Had he had a tipple when he let that slip a little?

But I'm almost muffled now. She has me pressed up against a wall, my head between her breasts like one or all of the three of us is going to give way to make fruit juice. A tipple... a nipple, even. Evening. Leaving.

Special dispensation. I plead inability, disability, gullibility. I've been too long in the hills, the smell and taste of a real woman is too heady a wine for my rarefied senses to refine. She puts me in the library like a book, in an inglenook, scaled by one of those little mobile ladders you only see in dreams.

And I sleep between several volumes of the Encyclopaedia Britannica keeping company for once with the truly great until my head hurts without a pillow, or is it the dreams of everything from A to Z and from Eden to Armageddon all strictly in order that do me in? At any rate, long before dawn, I'm gone. Down the treacherous dream-ladder and out through an Art Nouveau portal, slipping the bolt without a jolt, scared to wake her.

I sleep instead where I love, a more familiar bed, in the swaying fields of wheat not a hundred yards from Elissa's palatial abode, under a tree with the stars and the moon overhead, the only bed-mates I crave on a good day or a bad night.

In the morning Weasel wakes me, with Cynthia Beiderbecker at his side, just the ticket for a thicket, you can never find a retired occupational therapist when you need one, an occupational hazard-to-shipping in a sea of cereal, beached by the lighthouse. All those books and big ideas and bollocks. I let her ease my back with skilful hands while Elissa peers from on high from her parted voile curtains wondering what's ruptured, what we're up to, the three of us, what little's on show, with so much below, beneath the waves like golden hair on a summer's day, the sun like a wan face rising. Then it dawns on me as I glimpse her through her lacework windows moving about her corridors, pacing to and fro, that she has no head, only a glowing light, which all her flowing white dress flourishes and burnishes towards like the handle standard of a bed lamp. My false brother's lady is a false sun, a perambulating artificial illumination whose power fades by day, shamed by the sun she shuns so.

*

So. Just so. So so. -Is how I feel after my rough night, and too polite to complain or disclose my not-so-sweet repose amid the bibliophile delights of the best stocked library this side of Alexandria. I dare say. Cynthia and Weasel seem to have plans, designs on me even, hurrying me to the nearest hostelry to ply me with strong coffee and aromatic breads. I only manage a wave between two waves of ears of wheat, no tears to wit, to a distant window holding Elissa who sees me or not, in contempt or besotted, I know not as I depart her extensive policies. *Get knotted*, I propose to Weasel's infeasible insinuations that I should disclose the upshot and downdraught of the evening's ruminations. He thinks me coy and fey, offers to pay, but in fact I mostly can't remember.

This strategy returns dividends I see at the bank of mystique and mystery, as Weasel and Cynthia pull up their chairs to face me like inquisitors, suitors, executors. Exquisite silence then, eloquent as the sea, greets them, broken only by the happy lapping of me at my scrambled egg and toast soldiers. A shoulder to cry on, or two, between me and you, I can do without. Beyond doubt. And my eyes rise to catch a glimpse through the dusty coffee-room glass of the sudden sunlit patch of green on a hillside oddly wistful and distant in time and space. Already I long to return to the hills, escaping the race and the pills, the procrastination that fills the place for most people of what real life ought to be. *We've been thinking,* says Cynthia, *that you should play in our festival, your fiddle and whistle and all your fine wit, and maybe, just maybe, talk publicly and unpre-emptively, unprohibitively, unreservedly, just the littlest bit about that other, with whom you shared a mother, your brother: Zenir.*

Ahh, so that's what you're at! I laugh, then drinking, thinking how I could soon so easily grow to hate this man that I have never met, just by virtue of his supposed virtues which these numbskulls, pedants, peasants, pleasant dullards, unpleasant sycophants, psychopaths, sophomores, hyperbores and embryonic stalkers and poodle-walkers so constantly lick over like dying puppies with a fatal rash. It would be nice to unveil their hero as a pseud, a fraud, a bawd, a fallen god, if I could only find him and catch him off-guard, prise off his mask which he so surely wears as I wear mine. That… might be divine. And there may be time, but not now, for it seems my fate served up on a plate, irresistible as rashers, is to impersonate the dutiful brother, a quisling, sizzling, a ham, centre of attention, hot as I am.

It's a deal, we shake on it. The plates nearly break on it as Cynthia rises, tears of joy in her eyes, jolting the table. Fortunately I'm able to catch mushrooms in my maw like mice in a cat's paw or fish in a fat seal's muzzle, a veritable tussle, after which the café's morning crowd are laughing out loud. I'm doing them proud already and taking a bow, strafed by applause, which turns to nausea. This acting crap is easy but apt to make a tramp queasy who's eaten too fast and bent over moreover too quickly and jiggly, and now makes a dash to the bog. Fog of insight and delayed apprehension in the restroom mirror, forever too late: the incoming boat of wisdom, a bitter tide, the wrong side of the dawn, sour taste on the ever-flapping tongue. I wish I'd tethered it, leathered it. Outside once more, Weasel shows me the door and I bid gay good day to the first array of my fans, as he draws up his plans to use me, abuse me and hopefully lose me the moment he glances away.

So old Nadith is on the loose again with his antiquated boiler well stoked with animal fat, and I turn to Weasel as if waking up to ask: *What is this place called after all if anything at all?*

Suburbia, he says and it's hard to believe, indeed not just to leave when you hear that a town could exist with a communal imagination so depleted and degraded and frequently raided that it could anticipate and celebrate its own eventual incorporation and extinction into creeping polyunsaturated city-spread, so readily and clear-headily without even a flinch. We're walking the streets, Weasel and I, and now I'm asking him which town my supposed brother Zenir left to go to. *Industria,* he says, *way off to the west, and there to the south is the centre of it all, if there's a centre at all, the city of Urbis...* Foreboding, he points to it, far on the horizon, a collage of blocks and chimneys and steeples, a guddle of people, huddling together forever for warmth and anonymity and finding cold obscurity. Then quick as a flash he's drawing me a map, with chalk on a wall, worse than nothing at all, and the city it seems is surrounded by four quarters: *Suburbia, Industria, Oceania* and *Sylvia,* and Zenir has gone westwards like a clock hand moving backwards, and Suburbia is left behind here as high noon.

Just now someone cycles by and lets out a cry, it's Mary Winston her winsome smile turned to meet us with her eyes tight shut as seems to be the inevitable consequence of her entertaining a rictus on her visage, her body governed, automaton-like, by arcane archaic mechanical rules that her creator would rue were he even as lucid as me or you. *Nadith! Weasel! Good day!* –She declaims, waving sweetly, then crashes completely into a lamppost so upright and forthright as to brook no disagreement on the first law of thermodynamics, moreover showing cast-iron devotion to Newton's laws concerning bodies rest and motion. Crunch! Crumple! Emotion, concerned cries arise from all around the precinct and Weasel and I run to her aid. Too late, something uncanny has occurred we are appalled to discover as we grimace and hover, glimpsing over the shoulders of the jostling crowd as policeman Stout approaches with his gout and oversized breaches, blowing his whistle like a steam locomotive from a former age declaring war on the Beeching report. Mary and her bicycle, all blood and oil, cloth and rubber, are fusing, confusing and intermingling, impossible to single out from one another, becoming some new beast intent on cycling towards Bethlehem, dark and slouching if need be, but more likely smiling brightly in Mary's case, her face a spinning miasma of radial spokes with ears like handlebars. She's still alive, her heart beating, fed by oily chains, dynamos and metronomes, battery acid and elbow grease.

Mary dear! Hang on in there! -Weasel hails her as the ambulance wails and white-clad men arrive attended by bicycle engineers and a crack team of councillors briefed on post-traumatic stress disorder who fall on us all like vampire bats and we all scatter, escaping the splatter and novel collision of disparate matter demonstrated so ably by our lady friend the friendly librarian. Oh who will feed her books while she's away in hospital? Water them, index them? And what in turn, if not her healthy good books, shall sustain the ailing minds of the citizens of Suburbia, assailed nightly as they are by soap-opera atrophy and documentary entropy? – Curable only by cerebral endoscopy?

It's a poor show all round when you look at it like that, I conclude out loud to myself, *and we should tend lovingly to her library like a literary garden of Eden, or we're not half the men we think we are.* Then I remember that I am not *even* half the man Weasel thinks I am.

*

Gardening, that was it. My line of metaphoric reasoning before I fell asleep in a large planter basket in the main street, underneath some dahlias and chrysanthemums while Weasel foolishly abandoned me to go into a shop and buy matches. Have I been drunk, hung over? Moreover, why all the rhythm and rhyming, though not rhyme and reason? I feel better after the sleep of reason, no treason surely, but doubtless Officer Stout will Weasel me out if he catches wind of the caper. Enough! But look, it's John Joyce the gardener coming up to accost us now, I'd hoped that he'd lost us. That's three that I make, I've seen since, of the pontificant participants of last night's hallucinatory conference, left lurking in the mind. So they *were* real. JJ smiles, his long hair standing up like fronds of Phormium, baring his teeth and his secateurs, bringing us tidings of his first chore of the day, to go prune the roses of the good Doctor Tolleson. We best tag along says Weasel, a great tagger if ever there was one, and wasn't that how he found me? I owe him my name and purpose, breakfast and several drinks, but let's not toast those as virtues just yet until we've seen how this current embroilment boils out. Tagger and bagger, not to say tea-bagger. Mine's a lager.

Tolleson's lawn is wondrous green and lean, clipped to the bone like a forces crew-cut, criss-crossed by humming bees like droning B52s returning limping after flattening their floral Nagasakis. All sight-lines converge at the noble Georgian façade of his home: well-appointed, anointed, double-jointed and carefully re-pointed in a white lime putty made to a traditional recipe approved by the National Trust, involving horse hairs, neighbour's stares, builder's nightmares, and bullshit. Sandstone carved nudes and cast-iron rain-goods abound, and we're greeted and ushered to white metal patio chairs with floral cushions tied to them with little bows of ribbon that flutter in the breeze like flags and bonnets at a military parade. A tirade, first: we tell about Mary Winston's unfortunate accident, an incident in which we do not feel innocent, having caught her eye in the first place, and her having caught a lamppost in return, and now being hospitalised in an unfortunate indeterminate state between organic and inanimate matter at the molecular level, such as would confound even Heisenberg or Schrödinger were they to dare to take a look at her instead of her cat.

She doesn't have a cat, only books. -Weasel interjects at my verbalisation of this last perspective, compelling me to spray him with invective: *I'm quoting particle physics, quantum mechanics, dear boy, I'm sure the doctor's following me.*

Not in the slightest actually, Tolleson rebounds, taking off his glasses to rub them with his handkerchief, revealing the tiny vestigial eyes of a mole underneath.

Instead of looking at her pussy then, does that scan better or make more sense?

I tried that, by leering and angling, but she seemed to have a bicycle pump dangling...

Oh leave it, for God's sake. The point is, the poor woman will live, but suffice to say the next time you meet her you may feel uncertain whether to greet her or ride her.

Tolleson's eyebrows raise, now re-magnified in fishbowl haze. *My word, I've never thought of her like that. The wonders of modern medicine and their power to rejuvenate. Perhaps we should all try a collision with something mechanical now and again. I quite fancy a Penny Farthing or a moped.*

I see myself more as a Harley Davidson man, Weasel sighs, deflated somehow, set adrift on his own wistfulness. We all stare at the geraniums and delphiniums for a few minutes of happy vacancy, each to their own peculiar fantasy of machine-human hybrid.

Then John Joyce pipes up, hitherto weeding in the background, to say: *I would splice my genes to those of a rosebush any day. Plants do it with themselves and half the town without ever getting off their arses, do it with birds and insects too in a way. The dirty buggers.*

*Why roses though? —*Weasel ventures *—and risk getting pruned and beheaded all summer, a regular bummer. Why not a cedar or a yew, some a few millennia old so I'm told?*

Or a hedge? –I add, *hedges live forever, and so do we, if we could but look at it that way.*

Roses... JJ pauses and sniffs the wind, engorged of the beneficent spirit of creation, *-the most delicate, colourful, aromatic and alluring of beauties but defended like fortresses, they are love and death personified, rolled into one, the ultimate muses.*

Amusing... gentlemen, Tolleson nods like a sunflower in the wind, squinting, his twin glasses glinting. *You sound like to come back as a femme fatale would be your choice, Joyce.*

Yes, sir... he responds bending over, weeding and clipping, throttling and throttled, in a curious voice.

*

Next we find ourselves at Mary Winston's abode, let in by a pass-key kept under the door-mat, to water her books and read her plants to each other while she's away getting re-built as a bike. Or something like that. *Mary's library is even finer than Elissa's* –I pronounce, casting my eye about, *what a compassionate and passionate collection, indeed it gives me an erection.* A moment of reflection follows. The falling of dust motes through the hushed sunlight of the afternoon air, the grace of quiet interiors on hot days, distant birdsong from the garden, a sudden flash-fragment again of childhood memories, something about glimpses over neatly clipped hedges, orange squash and ice cubes on silver trays.

What did you just say? –Weasel puzzles, waking up from his tussles with a potted hyacinth over by the conservatory windows. *Crikey!* He suddenly looks startled, rattled. *Elissa actually showed you her library? That's quite an honour!*

Really? I slept in it, actually, on one of the shelves.

Weasel stops and looks at me in disgust and incomprehension. *Books are for reading, not using as pillows. Next you'll be telling me she showed you her...* There's a sudden extremely loud noise from the street at this, a car back-firing, after which I only hear the end of his scurrilous sentence *...put a plaster on it.*

What was that noise?

What? Oh that? That will just be Packer in his Studebaker.

What?

Classic cars, he loves them. Typical banker, too much money and too little imagination of what to spend it on. He'll have come to check on us, or on Mary's house, or both most likely.

What would you spend it on?

Me? Weasel pauses, smiling, showing a characterful gap in his rotting teeth, thinking but not taking long: *Parties and booze for all my mates, a happy throng, wine, women and song, laughter, partners for everyone, and a personal barmaid wearing only a thong.*

Imaginative. Ding dong. The door, the floor creaking under my feet on the way to answer it, glance at it: marvelling at the refraction of Packer's garish gold sweater and galoshes through the frosted glass. *Ahh, Packer, you ass!* enthuses Weasel over my shoulder, watering can in hand as they face up, man to man. *You look like Rupert The Bear in that ridiculous outfit, you and every other golfer!*

Packer is speechless, a rarity I guess, and turns to me for fresh perspective. *The most beautiful game in the world I'd say, and one of the oldest...*

Isn't that prostitution? Weasel drolls, returning to the kitchen.

...And an environmentally-friendly way of conserving vast tracts of land that might otherwise fall into the hands of rapacious property developers, wouldn't you say, Nadith?

Now, I don't know about that, I muse, aiming for amiable equanimity, *-and I must warn you that I prefer to be scrupulously truthful in my answers to such enquiries, not for the sake of community relations or abstract morality or a postulated deity, but because it gives me a watertight excuse for insulting people grossly. Golf, doing Nature a favour you say? Not quite, when humanity buggering off altogether would be an even greater one. On my many enormously long walks across every mile of this country I have often found myself unwelcome and shouted at as I was driven to violate the pristine greenness of some pointlessly banal sterile landscape dedicated to the insipid gods of golf. And the outfits... and the little carriages... and the vast array of clubs like a dentist's tools, why, it is human idiocy made manifest,* *so resplendent even as to verge surely on self-parody. In which case, come to think of it, I'm all for it. You're a travelling clown I see now, attired therefore appropriately. I greet you excitedly and expectantly as a schoolchild and await to be entertained by your tricks. Unhook your floppy braces. May I take your red nose and fill it with tea?*

Ha ha ha, very laconic and sardonic... chuckles Packer.

Moronic... echoes Weasel from afar.

I heard that. I'm a banker you know, an iconic Ionic pillar of the establishment, a trusted thrusting member of this community.

A clown, juggling other people's money more like. A huckster, a trickster... Weasel fumes coming back into the room.

Now now, my friend, if you had any money, and weren't nearly a tramp, then I would be looking after it for you and doing great things for you with it, doubling your returns, speculating and accumulating.

Expectorating... Weasel interjects, *I will be soon, as a well-known precursor to vomiting.*

*Now now **now**,* Packer claps his large hands with disturbing hairs on their backs reminding me of King Kong swatting aeroplanes, calling everyone to order, *just listen to ourselves in front of our new friend Nadith, what kind of example are we setting? Is this not in fact the very measure of the value of our Secret Skygazers Club, that people so diverse as you and I, from every weird walk of life can find ourselves together of an occasion disagreeing agreeably over the exact nature and niceties of things? And didn't our one deranged and unknowable God make all of us as his daft little toys in the hope that we would all be good and play nicely together when he laid us out on his floormat and shoved us around putting on silly voices? And look at us here, all hurrying together to help out our recently injured friend out of concern for her and her property.*

Property? Weasel unwinds, defused like a truck bomb. *Our friend Nadith here has even less property than me. Not even a home, other than his own body, and at times he seems to be only renting even that from an absentee slum landlord. Isn't that right?*

Righter even than you know, I affirm with a nod of my snout, and seeing my doubt, Packer leaps into the breach: *Listen, my friend, I've heard things, indeed great things, about your abilities to theorise and proselytise, appetise and anaesthetise, on the abject subject of your famous brother's inspiration, his inclination, propitiation, preparation, initiation and substantiation for his expensive and expansive canvases, his paintings apt to cause faintings and fits of hysterical adoration in pubescent girls. Would you be willing to do same, and speak publicly about him, on a big wooden platform adorned with colourfully striped party buntings, in front of the whole populace of our charming little town? Popcorn may be involved.*

I try to argue, but am beset by fate in the form of a maniacal hacking coughing fit, from which my voice emerges hoarse, saying: *Anything of course, for a charming little clown.*

*

Cynthia Beiderbecker finds me brooding in the old churchyard, dappled with the tiger-stripes of shifting shadows of leaves of ancient trees, communing, attuning, afternooning on the mossy slabs with my wires plugged in to yesteryears, a jester's tears. *Who on earth sunbathes on grave slabs?* –She exclaims, *you are a rum fellow, Nadith, who does not feel the chill of death and shiver at its solemn insinuations.*

Insinuations, implications... I mutter *...bold, emboldening implications if you once cease your flight from fear and stand your ground, turn around to think things thoroughly through. And we should do, each of us, me and you.*

How so? –She pauses, wrong-footed, wrong-headed. She must have seen me over the dry stone wall, her cranium floating disembodily by on the way to ordering her supposedly retired limbs around to a not-so-pressing, perhaps depressing, appointment. Instead of which, as if faintly fascinated, she now sits down on the green mossy velvet cushion of this ecclesiastical lounge. Pull up a pew.

Each single life must begin and end, but the threads of lives of which we are made lead outward from this point in every direction, escape detection, forward and back in time, like the reins of a galloping mare, if you will, which we hold in our hands. And yet, we fail to see this power and chance, clutching but weakly for our day in the saddle, dither and addle, rarely seizing the crop or the spur. We are more than ourselves it seems, is what I mean to say. We can reach out and touch those who came before and who will come hereafter, know them intimately, and their company is a comfort, warm not chill.

Cynthia, eagle eyes wide, spies my wires and wonders. *You're not just talking about nippers and wrinklies, are you? You're reading the stones somehow, is that what you're at? Can you, could you, show me what you see?*

Alas, I sigh, *for that, you would have to shear all your lovely golden locks like the fleece of a lamb, as have I.* I take my long mop of peppery grey and black tramp's hair in both hands and lift it right off its Velcro patches, and hand it to Cynthia, savouring the shock that stops her talk. Tick tock, a penny drops, she looks from wig to bald head and bald head to wig again, marvelling at the mass of electrode patches, neural nexus of flexes from neck to crown, temple to auricle. Oracle, hard-wired in the electronic age, but tuned to every other one. Her mouth is a great 'O', trembling and quivering at the threshold of gnosis, neurosis, pondering what form to take for its next incantation, prayer or lament. She opts, wisely perhaps, for humour:

I've been wondering how you kept it so clean. A quick dip in the sink and your all-weather polyethylene mane is brand new. A toupée which has duped a fellow or two, no doubt. Now tell me, what do all those wires do?

They convey to my serene cerebellum and amiable amygdalae the signals that the wires in my frayed and foppish cuffs take in. The hypnotic trance state, a quirk of fate, is a rare but distinct pattern in human neurological activity. Years ago, I recorded and mapped it in a clairvoyant subject, an obliging patient, who shaved his head thus to allow this cranial apparatus so to be applied. My contraption, as I disarmingly think of it, has recreated that state on my bald pate on demand ever since, weaving and leaving an electromagnetic field around me that forces my brain into receivership. Then all I need do, is find some stimuli, traces of past and future lives, recorded in stones.

Holy help, Cynthia yelps, *this is like a smoke, a toke, sold by some dodgy bloke, of something Lebanese purchased in Amsterdam. You were a doctor of medicine before? A weighty scientist of some arduous discipline?*

I think so... perhaps...my memory comes and goes like April showers.

As a result of the... contraption? Like some freelance tramp's trepanning, you've damaged or altered yourself by using it too much, or such and such, over the years, to the point of tears?

I shake my head. *I don't think so... but it's hard to be sure, to be sure, of anything anymore. Except what I see, which is people from history and from the other place...*

Other?

White, always white, and silver. Dashing around in anti-gravitational gyrations and incomprehensible incoherences. The futurists, the ones who will doubtless, redoubtably, come after.

But only stones? You said stones permit, transmit and store these signals, nothing else, not metal or wood nor plants and trees or birds and bees?

It's a peculiarity of the illogical atomic, not to say, anatomical logic of stone, like a vinyl record scored by a needle or a tray of silver nitrate exposed to bright light. Metal's no use for the trick, electrons go straight through it, but stone alters every time, under the right conditions, it records.

What? You're talking about ghosts are you not? The supernatural? Just what are the right conditions to mint, to imprint, ourselves into stone?

Stress, sadness, terror, horror, despair, the moments when the human spirit tries hardest to depart from the body, and it seems that it succeeds, leaving its mark in the dark, a kind of distress beacon that resonates across the waves of the sea of time. Oh yes, and thunderstorms and lightning-struck days, by chance, will do it too, like making milk curdle in a pail, not just an old wives' tale.

And what were you watching on this psychic television of yours before I chanced by? Cynthia smiles, convinced perhaps of my evinced clairvoyancy, buoyancy bobbing on the seas of time, or more likely humouring a man with a brain tumour, probably.

And I so nearly tell her, to dispel her sceptic demeanour. But just then, one chance in ten, her spouse a mouse the male of the species Beiderbecker Eiderpecker comes trailing by as my hairpiece settles back down onto my Velcro crown. I see he's a cardigan which dreamt it was once a man, or a strawberry flan. Now I'm shaking his hand like an elastic band stretching tight to propel me upright until I let go and brace for the blow, expecting one of us to fire away and roll in the grass like a prize ass. Rollover and take it, man, you're a wino, a dino, supplanted, superseded, succeeded by a weed in tweed, who has all that you need without knowing. My heart bleeds.

*

The pub beckons I reckon, my money-less method of procurement of nourishment, continue the punishment. Just throw me a fiddle again, fine gents and dear ladies, and let me dispense with a ladle the hot broth of music, the froth which doth (he quoth) replenish the soul and dispel all hell's demons. And after you have each and all been served well so shall I, like a servant in the basement quarters, receive my plate of ritual victuals, pie beans and chips served up with a quip from Clarissa the trusty and busty barista. *Dusty!* She proclaims and swishes and blushes with her shiny shammy while we all hoist our beverage headwards until the saloon typhoon has blown through. *Your music was so lovely, Nadith,* she croons, winking, *now for an encore, what shall you do?* The old Joanna tinkles under my pinkies, ebonies and ivories, sweets and savouries, like Jonah in the whale I lose myself and earn myself a pudding, toffee and clotting cream.

A clapping of hands and clearing of throats and clearing of tables. I turn to see it's Tolleson emerged like a circus ringleader from the esoteric backroom to announce tomorrow evening's big attraction, that Nadith shall be giving an intellectual lecture on the work of his brother the great artist Zenir Learmot, and isn't that simply marvellous? And certainly it will be, if I can summon up anything half convincing to say about a man I wouldn't know from Adam, Cain, or Abel. But hark, the silky Cynthia slides down to my table, gliding from somewhere to sit by my side. Then I see Heaney and Packer, dispersing and mingling to chatter too, they've all been unleashed, from the weird light at the end of the room and the world, from an afternoon's gazing up the rectums of celestial spectres. Etcetera. *And rumour has it,* Tolleson adds, as a spicy afterthought, *that the renownedly reclusive Lady Elissa herself may be joining us for the occasion.* Amazing. This seems to tickle the whole room who rise to the vocation and strike up a tune. Someone else's turn sawing the strings and vibrating the reed, now I'm up on my feet being spun like a bobbin on the golden threads of Cynthia's hair and smiles, a nicer place than Elissa's sickly lair.

And over her shoulder I spy Weasel returned to the fold, conferring with Heaney and Packer, discussing me over glowing pints of amber, my mood edges blacker, remembering I've seen the sum total of three paintings by the brother I've never met or known. Yet I must praise or denounce him, bless or wound him by cutting my own scrap of fame off the end of his robe, to feed with myself to the dogs. My mind fogs at the prospect, less appealing than sleep. The sheep, time to leave their fold.

Outside this time, night time. The right time. Under the sailing and regal moon in her gossamer negligee of clouds blowing white light like cold fire, ancient watchful eye remembering all that we forget again and again across ages and aeons. And there, like a prayer, suddenly, is Cynthia quietly by my side. *And what did you really see today in the churchyard, Nadith? Tell me, whisper it, unravel it for my ears, unlock the years, let me have it, the present of travel to the non-present, conundrum which may end in madness or tears.*

And in this quiet street we walk through, how all the trees and bushes and hedgerows seem hushed and hunched over like monks in hoods immersed in green hymns, asleep in their pews, the timber fences of suburbia which keep them confined and subdued. Here the roadway is steep and my heart slows, and all my fear of life drains and goes. Fear of life, yes that's right, not of death, for throughout all my lonely existence and travels it is them, those spectres of life gone and life to come that have sustained me, thrilled me with their light. But it is the hot breath and beating heart of another living being which terrifies me most, a penetrating stare straight to my heart, seeking me out where I can no longer hide, hermit crab deprived of his shell. My fingers sweat, my pulse and heartbeat race, oh not because I am cold as many think, but the opposite, so much the opposite that I can never speak it or explain, but long to confess and take off this mask which chokes me every breathing second. I am in pain.

Here at the head of the hill, I seize Cynthia by the shoulders and press my cheek against her ear and hope that she can see what I see, as I turn her around to face her little town while my dial rotates and the voltage buzzes, my wires sizzling against her nails, her hair standing on end. *There is where you played as a child the day the carnival came to the town, late summer with thunder in the sky, the players going by, the clowns on their wagon, the tattooed lady, the midgets, the trapeze, the beautiful white pony cantering with disciplined legs. And here years later at the next corner, is where you saw your little brother struck by a blue sports car driven by a lady with silver hair tied back with a red bandana...*

Horrified, Cynthia spins away like a top released from my maelstrom, ricocheting off moonlit fences and hedges in dismay and confusion. *Who told you all this? −My intimate secrets, what brigand has sold you my past at what price?* Her eyes blaze orange, brimming with stinging hurt. *Who are you?*

I recoil and cringe at her vituperation, however expected and inevitable, however many times witnessed before, wanting to cover my face with the cage of my fingers and hide and hide. *No...* I must defend myself, even though the denying words themselves somehow sully me, brand me with some vague crime. *All that I speak is divined, gleaned from the air and the stones, from the windows that open for me that show me glimpses through time. Trust me, believe me, I can prove it to you a hundred times over unless your mind is closed, in which case all is in vain. Did you not see it yourself as I held you?*

I, I... she ventures to speak, but stumbles, her eyes searching inside herself, uncertain, her life's whole sober foundations quaking mirage-like, brushed away by a sorcerer's hand. She finds herself on the edge of a cliff which no man can see, for it extends inside herself, offering her the chance to be free, but which gripped by fear she sees as death in some sly disguise. Which it is not, but the opposite. Deathlessness, the realisation of the continuum of which we are part, stitched in forever, safe, bound. Found.

Unable to cope, tearful, fretful, her lip bitten and quivering, she runs away, turning back and back, again and again as she wends her way, her long hair swinging like a pendulum, metaphor for the human soul tormented by memory and regret unable to look forward. I watch her dwindle down the dimming alleyway towards her house and know that I and the moon are to be wretched companions again under the stars for one more night in this unfathomable universe.

*

My dreams come swift and terrible, of edible horses of candy arrayed in a bay of white sugary sand, dissolved by frothy tides of lager shandy, chewing at each other's limbs while they play in the waves until the cannibalism turns nasty. The sea turns red but I can't turn my head away, and then regiments of pork pies parachute out the skies pursued by black flies with the faces of ex-lovers. I want to switch this dream for another, a power usually granted me but on this occasion suspended. I float out to sea until my boat pie is upended, and I clutch to the edge of it like a raft, along with two Edwardian ladies dressed in white meringue and a minister all in black and white who I begin to suspect is made of liquorice, so quickly does he melt in the sun. His moustached face frightens me so I hide underneath the ladies' dresses and pressing my head to their intimate places find the taste of cinnamon.

*

Next day in a pile of hay she finds me, by what way I know not how, for I thought I'd concealed my miserable tracks well enough, through some hedge and bush to an untended acre at the edge of the town's river. *Nadith, Nadith, how can you sleep outdoors like this? It is too terrible, too pitiable, you must sleep in the spare room we have over our garage in the spare blankets and pillows we keep there...* Her mouth and sweet breath are close to my ear, her hand on my chest, my heart still calm and methodical as a tolling bell, from all its travels through the wellsprings of sleep, undersea currents of dreams.

And what I wonder, I waken and blunder, *will your spouse make of a mouse concealed in his loft like a maggot in an apple, wriggling its way nightly to the sweet core? Do not pity me, please, I am not worth it. A tramp, a down-and-out, a scallywag, a ne'er-do-well limping his slow sad way to hell. I can survive hunger and cold but pity, spare me that, only that can do me in. It's dignity that keeps me and every other creature walking, and the likes of me can only maintain theirs by shutting out everybody else's shitty view of their shitty state. Although I am prepared to concede, that in diluted form, I might just have coincidentally described and circumscribed everybody else's fate there too.*

Nadith, do not speak disparagingly, dismissively of yourself anymore. I am sorry for all that I said with the winds of last night blowing through my dishevelled head. I could not handle what you offered me, and though I still can't, I have slept on it a whole night now, and with the bright morning light it strikes me that what I saw and heard are a wonder not a terror, and that you are an angel, an agent, of something good, and not of that dark other. Make me your friend. I am your sister, brother.

And there for a moment in the dawn light, she unbuttons my shirt and touches the dial upon my chest, the raw puckers and tears of red flesh, the marks of tape and glue, the numerals and increments, puzzling over what they do. I am the supple shuttle of the present, master of the warp and weave, the bobbin through which the loom of time speaks, threading and knitting and sewing all past and future into my fabric, my soul. Cynthia kisses me once on the mouth, a moment of infinite possibility and promise, as vital as the sun, then hurries away, promising to meet me at the library at two.

*

Before that, there's Weasel chasing me to help out in another garden errand with JJ and broom and rake and secateurs. On a salubrious side of town in an enviable gown of greenery and preenery, a mammoth hedge is ready it seems to be pruned and sculpted by a master with a ghetto-blaster. Radio on, JJ sets about it derangedly with enormous shears, deafening the ears of neighbours while we, his collaborators, beat time like vibrators, sweeping up clippings and chipping them into huge sacks of Hessian as part of an elaborate impromptu dance. Paid in advance, we don't envisage a chance of curtailment of this entertainment, until Heaney trots by with news of derailment, bids us look up at the sky. Rain on the way, lads, and trouble brewing.

He offers us cigarettes and the sour taste of regrets, sitting down to rest on a fence. *Always check the weather report before you commence. And don't get into things that you don't mean to complete, eh, Nadith? Like talking sweet to another man's woman?* What? I object to this rumour! But humour him, playing it down to the ground ready for sweeping, keeping my secret anger and shame, even to hear him speaking her name.

Then JJ laughs in comic conclusion, supplanting threat with the illusion of harmony, bidding us guess the design in relief which his shears have half-created out of branch and leaf. Can you see what it is yet? Kismet. Traces of two lovers' faces in kissing embraces. But perhaps it is all Rorschach ink blotting rather than anyone plotting. No time to learn what anyone else is seeing anyway. For next rain begins falling, in big drops, fat, splat, black as any ink. Heaney, heinous, intravenous doomsayer, you have found your calling. Nose up. We mere men can dry out later, but the ghetto-blaster, inspired to rise to the challenge of its nickname, hisses and blows up.

*

I wait outside the library, which doubtless would not admit me were it not for who will come in with me: Cynthia, sliding, gliding down the road to meet me, a smile swimming in her eyes, glinting with the sunlight. She puts a motherly arm around me and ushers me in, through the ancient hardwood spinning doors, the deep smells of dust and furniture polish, over the ornate floor tiles speaking of the orient and Arabia, of the great lost days of empire.

Cynthia asks the staff for the maps, and when they come rolls them out proudly, huge and ancient across the ornately carved table, filling the air with motes of fine dust in the fingers of light from the skylit lantern sailing high overhead at the intersections of plaster carvings and pillars and pendentives. A grand old space for a daft little town. All yellow and brown: these ancient charters. *A Roman wall ran here,* she says, *right through the churchyard where you described it, and a monastery stood here likewise where also you clapped eyes on ghosts of times departed. And you're telling me you've never seen these records, that you knew this only by mysterious illumination?*

Divination. Second sight as some have dubbed it long since before now in centuries gone. An inherited glitch, which I have enhanced and accentuated by electromagnetic tricks. Nothing new under the sun. But better than that, better yet, Cynthia, I can read you the map that has not yet been drawn, can see the view beyond this present dawn. All these houses here for instance, will be bulldozed and this road re-routed through here where I point. And machines beyond your understanding built on this hill in vast phalanx like silent white armies to power the city of Urbis which will crawl from the horizon yet further until it kisses right here, eating and drinking at the beloved river that nurtured your town.

Can you show me such wonders, with my own eyes? —She marvels, and I grow afraid and timid of the spark I see I have lit, the dangers therein which she can't guess yet. Her golden hair weaves the celestial light in that bibliophile hush, and I shrink from the gush of future which assails me. I raise a hand to her tresses, it distresses me, the price my trans-temporal device exacts of a mortal. Nadith, Nadith, throttle your desire.

A distraction, man of action. Take me, Cynthia, to the sections displaying newspapers and books of contemporary art. *I must learn by heart the works of my brother to satisfy my audience and their thirst for titbits on his greatness, his lateness, he who has blazed through this town like a comet and left so much adulation, dazed in his wake.*

And at length we find him, his photo portraits, the trickster and huckster, self-promoting at functions and luncheons, and in the background his works lurking and towering, over-powering, dominating the feeble-minded who cannot dream for themselves and need his lead to look into the next world where the faerie flag unfurls. Uncurling, serpent Zenir slithers through the contours of their bowels, lengthening their vowels, promoting their taste for pretension, distancing themselves from each other by claims they can lay to his vision, acquisition in material transposition of the spiritual windows he opens. They clutch his frames, the curtains, fixate on names, missing the message, the space in between all that they can contain with their slippery fingers, while he runs free, rich as I am poor. Let them sniff and lick at his spoor. I spy the sky in which he flies, and I shall climb cloud by cloud and catch him there.

*

Tonight is the night, the moment just right. The moon waning from its fullness, the game up, time for the new order of things I bring, ring ring as churchbells tolling. The village hall, in front of them all, the hordes of Suburbans, I must hold forth on Zenir. Tolleson stands to do the inducting, introducing, educating, electrocuting us all with his rapier patter on ecumenical matters. While I sit on the podium I caress a dark varnished wood baluster, letting its time flow up my sleeve and show me Victorian tourists in black powdery dresses and oily tresses traversing the room in chilling transparency as Tolleson's words echo to vacancy. *We are very honoured to have here tonight to speak to us, Nadith Learmot, esteemed brother of the renowned oil painter Zenir. Nadith will offer us insights into the creative process of his brother and indeed what it means to grow up so close to so talented an other with whom one shares a mother. He may even go further and tell us how his own musical style on the fiddle and whistle is an aural acoustic component, an alternate exponent of the same deranged muse, of self-awareness, self-exploration, and self-abuse. Enough! My tongue has got loose and lacerated the patient ears of my best audience in years. I am brought nearly to tears, and the occasion has scarcely even farted. I give you, Nadith Learmot, journeyman and musician, rhymer and out-of-timer, seer without peer unaged by his years...*

I stand like a tornado rising from the dry plain, gathering and looming over prairies of ripe wheat. The pale pasty indoor faces before me shrink from the shadow I throw, and like a wolf among the chickens I go. *Zenir Learmot is a charlatan!* I proclaim. *A mischievous demon who has deceived your eyes and your ears over many sorry years. His talent mediocre compared to his gifts of self-promotion and proclamation, promulgation of his own personal myth, which you all like silly sheep repeatedly buy into.*

People begin to titter, then laugh whole-heartedly. Oh what a jolly jape to ape a disgruntled critic when we all know you are an ardent fan, they muse, a ruse of rhetoric and repartee designed to bring us all guffawing to our knees. Why do they think I am joking? Am I dressed as a clown, in a golf outfit perhaps, like Henry Packer, with my buggy and clubs parked outside? Clubs, yes, I might be needing those soon.

Look at these daubs! I shout, holding a few library books up. *You so want to believe that this daft little country produces great art and artists, I understand that completely, but you are looking in the wrong places. This man is a cartoonist, a lampoonist, a harpoonist of the great white whales of modern art who passed this way and sank beneath the waves, Picasso, Beckman, Matisse, over fifty years ago now, and who knows if their like will ever surface again. But if they did, you certainly wouldn't notice! He is not recording or dignifying contemporary life, he is caricaturing and cheapening it, laughing at you all while you give him your money and misplaced adulation, reputation in spades, but it fades... it fades, my friends, and history makes its true judgement in due course. It judges you for all the other figures you passed by and left in the shadows, struggling for their whole lives for an audience and a living wage. It has been ever thus, as history books attest, but I protest, here and now, to your faces, and I accuse you each for the shallow fools you are. I am the voice of history, a tramp who wanders the wilderness from town to town, but browned by the sun, I live in truth while you live in pale white lies. That is my gift, the gift I offer you, more valuable than all your money and possessions, the materialist trinkets you surround yourselves with like children's toys.*

The laughter has been gradually thinning out, discomfort fermenting in twitching arms and legs and hands and feet. Then something happens, the door at the back opens, and a blinding yellow light floats in with a long white dress beneath it. It is Elissa, lighthouse of suburbia turning all their heads, dazzling, confusing, blinding... yes... even me. I stumble, I stutter, something changes, I have to keep talking but lose track of my thread, my own words. I hear myself continuing to speak, but no longer recognise my voice or understand it:

Yes, it is true. I grew up with him. I remember him painting and drawing, just as I was always writing and making music, since we were old enough to stand. Can you imagine what it is like to share a bond like that? We read the same books, marvelled at the same stories and films. We fantasised together, created our own shared imaginative universes, even our own language, made-up words. We knew deep down that we would both conquer the world one day, each in our very different ways. And so we have. I am hidden while he is seen. He appears to be understood, while in fact is universally misunderstood. I appear to be misunderstood, as if a failure, a penniless tramp, but in fact I am understood only too well by all those who turn away and try to forget and ignore me. He appears to be rich, but he is lonely and trapped and frightened within the fragile glass palace that you and he have built for him. He appears to be rich, but I am free and so I am the richer. His star will fall, but mine will never falter... He was a great artist once, not least when we were children together, but your adulation has destroyed him, corrupted him into self-parody.

Tears seem to be welling up in my eyes, but whether of emotion or simple reflex, my eyes smarting, I am unable to decide. The light from Elissa's head seems to be blinding me and the whole room, throwing everything before me into shadow. My words are petering out now... *What... what's happening? Can somebody tell me... I don't seem to be able to see anything any more...*

Then as quickly and mysteriously as it first happened, the yellow light blinks out as Elissa stoops and leaves discreetly by a side door, which is left open for a moment before a new apparition rolls in: Mary Winston or what used to be Mary, some living fragments thereof most certainly, but rebuilt and subsumed into a bike, a trike, a shrike, a fright of machinery and person intertwined. Wheels lifting and turning, pistons churning, her cheeks burning, facial expressions twisting, forehead puckering in gathering of abstruse literary thoughts garnered and nurtured in the infinite shelves of a lifetime's libraries. Mary has become erudition manifest at last, borne on the sweet waft of foosty paper, a carefully substantiated and cross-referenced theory with footnotes, that only dreamt it was a woman, only a pale worm left behind like a thing spilled from an anatomist's pickling jar, broken on the wheel of learning. And crucified now on the spokes of a bicycle.

The audience love it. Uproarious applause and spontaneous outbursts and ululations. Whether at my errant ruminations or the safe return of Mary Winston to their warm bosom from the attentions of engineers and surgeons, I know not, nor care a jot. I turn to leave behind this lot, all chatting, scatting, platitudinous platypuses clapping and snapping their beaks open and shut to void their gullets, their glut of gelatinous gossip which drips weakly in ooh-ahs and tut-tuts. All mates and darlings like chattering starlings. They're moving on to the pub, Weasel and JJ and Packer and Cynthia's hub' who does like a tipple he stipulates on weekday nights only and mixed with soda in a cup. Meanwhile I catch his wily wife's eyes and retire by a back door to the sight of night skies, the myriad stars curving over as we retreat down the street in strangely tacit deceit, the world at our sweet feet.

Oh how to describe her kiss in the dark of her doorway? Her leading hand in the hush of her stairway? Kneeling in the attic like abasing myself before the altar of the sky, where her telescope rests aimed at the stars. Unwrapping her clothes like the gift of the present: sweet musk of cloth on fragrant flesh, the taste of her nipple in my mouth, succour given by mothers to men, eternal dispensation lost and forgotten in the daily rush, the masked ball of banality we rise to each morning, donning our costumes like clowns doomed to futility, voluntary insanity. Her tongue in my mouth, our reaching out to insert each tentative tentacle into available orifices. Creatures fusing, confusing, losing the boundaries of the disparate worlds our hearts push blood to in tides. Oh where does it reside? Your soul, Cynthia, as I push you upwards to heaven, the distant frightened creature sliding away behind your eyes, timid, blind, wondering what it rushes and yearns towards, not just now, but all of its life? Wondering who I am, this stranger, and who you are, made stranger still. It kills us, this moment of thrill, not for itself but the window it offers of infinite possibilities of escaping the flesh and transcending the will.

It's over as ever too soon, but I'd swear that time stopped there just for a moment and eternity lived in the space of one breath and half a shared heartbeat. Shall we be discreet? Shall we speak when we meet? Or look down at our feet? None, for now, let us sleep, entwined on the floor with clothes strewn around and half off us like broken chains, escaped slaves careless of the wrath of their master, distant thunder vibrating the horizon as the reed of a hunting horn. Scorn, shame, infamy, doubtless await us, but for now joy, exhilaration placates us.

*

And when is it we wake? The chasm, the break, when self-consciousness floods in on the children of Eden? Suddenly he's there, Eiderpecker on the stairs, crying and swearing and lifting handfuls of blonde hair up in his hands, his eyes bulging in unbelieving, his senses leaving him. All this the price of just four rounds of beers. And there I am: still clutching the incriminating scissors, standing proudly over his lady wife, my pupil who sits naked and entirely bald on her chair at the telescope, with my net of electrodes spread over her scalp like a hair net, asking *Are we there yet?* -as I lead her voyaging through the landscape of past and future years. This was doomed, of course, to end in tears. She hasn't even heard him yet, so locked is she in the vista of her transfigured town from this privileged loft, with time pulled aside like a curtain, satin soft. She turns and their eyes meet and his throat erupts in wails that rotate my entrails. I decide to depart before all that entails. He raises a hand, attempts harm, assails, misses, flails, caught unawares. I dart down the stairs then off out into the night, out of sight and out of mind of all of my kind.

*

And so it is over. As so often before. And out into the loving roving wilderness I go, fleeing all that is behind me, eloping with my sweet soul, hoping that none shall follow or find me. And nothing binds me. I live outside their grid, without money or cards or papers, or even a name which I can't dispose of. How I have loathed *Nadith*, and look forward to another. I will seek out my brother and see what he names me or defames me in retribution for my stain on his reputation. I doubt any such disputation, seriously now, there must be some compensation for my diminution, tiny fly who crawls through all the muck of the world, sustained thereby.

Walk on, walk on. Tick tock, the implacable clock of time talks on, but I am going out of hearing. Nearing enlightenment by dint of each weight I shed, led by my nose, struck as my heart has bled, the clothes of affection left dying in their unmade bed, sorrow I shall not disclose even to myself. Rumour of love lost behind me, pining in repose.

Cynthia's sweet smells still enclose me, winding and intertwining as invisible threads about me in the air and everywhere. I shall not seek to wash, but rain no doubt shall shower my body soon enough and roughly scourge this old brain, purge it of its amorous aspirations and all its vain hopes of acceptance anywhere, gurgling down the drain.

Suburbia's tarmac fades out from beneath my feet until I meet the moor, and gaining height there after hours look back, content to have concealed my spoor. That little town is littler still now, small enough to hold in my hand and understand one day, should I choose to turn my mind back there. I sigh goodbye and take to the track and walk for hours, leaving my shadows behind, each peeling off with the passing trees, my memories going with them, like discarded clothes or skins, a peeling onion man, this accounting for the tears in my eyes, should anyone wonder. Fat chance, distant thunder, who but me walks in these domains today far from the living? Come the rain, fat drops forgiving in rapturous baptismal blessing, purge me clean.

At nightfall I chance upon a dark lake in a hollow, large and elliptical, swirling in purple shadow reflecting the blushing watercolour sky, and I stop with a start, struck to the heart, seeing its true form: a vast eye, black pupil rotating at it centre, seeking me out. And I sit down on a rock at the edge of the woods which smudge its shore like an eyebrow, fearful of this apparition, full of contrition. Then behind me footsteps I hear, thinking them imagined, clear out my ears and shake my head. Wish myself dead. But they're there and gaining volume and ground, someone running, pursuing me from town. I reach up my fingers to my face and they linger, finding the trace of my true nature I forgot. Just a flick and twist and I've got it, the whole lot, off in my hands, my mask, my false face, just metal mirror again, reflecting the leaves dark and green above me. I turn smiling to greet the stranger, and it's Weasel, mouth open, about to speak, convinced he has found me at last, but aghast, hovers, bereft as a lover, unable to complete the sentence he's framed, until shamed, confused, disabused of his illusions, he turns to retreat the way he came, and plods off, slow and distraught, disappointed in deed, deep in thought.

Another hour on, light gone, I bed down. I wash my face in the water and kick off my boots, lay my head back among the roots and leaves in the green bosom of trees and sleep, dreaming of naught.

~

PART TWO

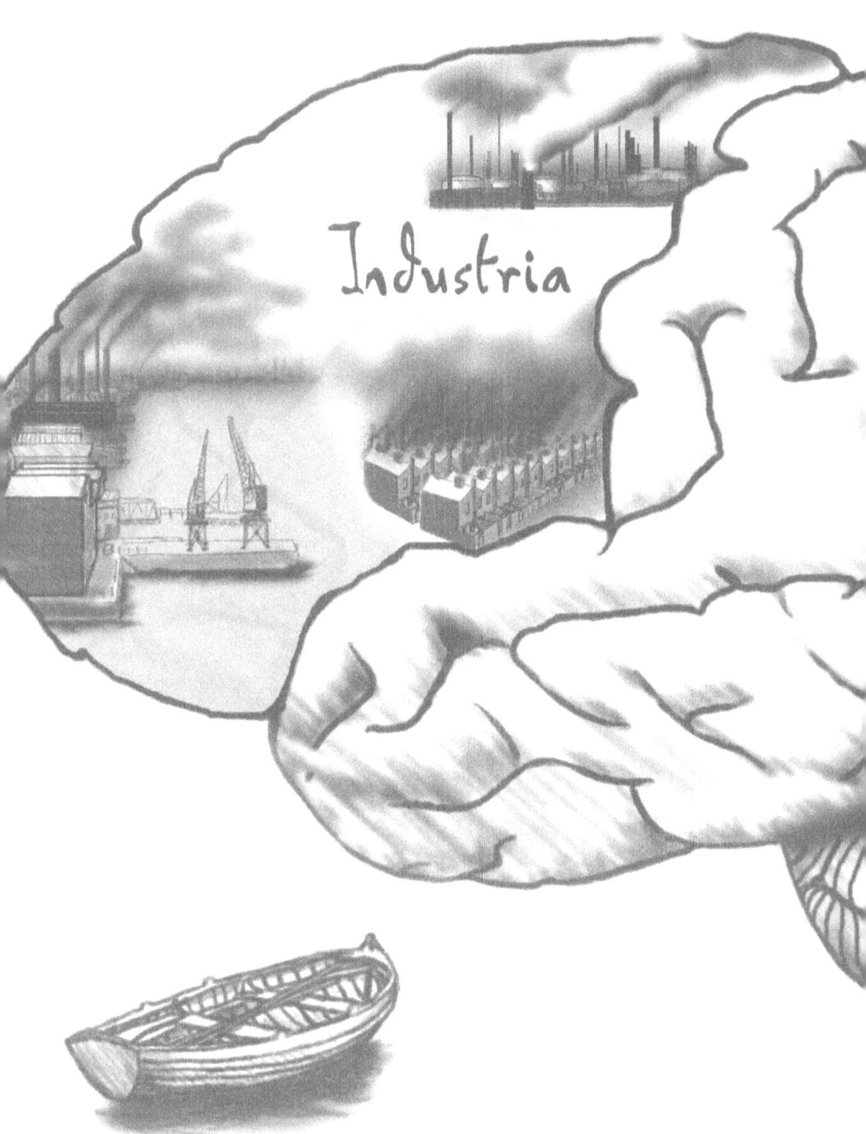

Industria

Such greyness and stillness I wake into today, as if all of Nature is pausing, loath to go on, suspending Her charade, Her masquerade. This weariness I feel also in my limbs, and on a whim I swim in the lake instead, water up to my head, and am reborn from the dead, freezing and shaking, shocked and blue as the newborn emerging, howling and crying, with only grass and air for towelling and drying, my clothes hanging from trees. And these I wash now, slow as I please, teasing out every last atom of dirt and scent of the words I meant and those I did not, the lot, thrown to the breeze. My past is shed, my chapter read, time to head to pastures fresh.

The sky still so still, static as a grey sheet, but neat, complete as a new white page for writing. But as I walk on I see that autumn is encroaching, curling the leaves at the edges, whispering in hedges of death and decay. But unlike human dismay, Nature delights like a sunset in this phase of her work, the glorious hues soon to be unleashed, gold, orange, pink, brown and red. She celebrates her dead, sends them off in a fanfare of brass trumpets of crumpled and crinkled leaves and fronds. Fond but unsentimental, knowing what we cannot grasp within the petty spans of our lives and shuttered minds, that time and tides bring back all things washed clean, renewed in the green font of rebirth, a cold fusion, remarkable oven fed by dead flesh and broken dreams. Rejoice therefore that our failures are fodder in the grand scheme that redeems our every ounce, cry out in joy as we are trounced. We are not undone but remade, over and over again, and since of necessity not least our minds must be washed, be not surprised that our memories are quashed also in this forge that gorges itself on the rich food of our endeavours. Severed we seem, as roots by the rake, but deeper beneath the earth spread the wiser tendrils that unite us with our children and all the next of our kind, out of sight, out of mind. Few can encompass this vista, but who do, are truly awake.

I cover so many miles. I should be aiming away from Urbis, that distant city crouched on the horizon and its sorry suburbs spread out around it and below me, like the fans and folds of some vast skirt. I should be away to the west and the open sea, the myriad islands, the mild climates warmed in the gulf, or to the high moors and fierce peaks to the north, bitter as gritted teeth which seethe with the bloody history of those born in their lee. But somehow, like a ball on a string, or a hunting hawk loosed from his master's gloved hand, whichever trajectory I conceive, deceives, and I find myself curving back towards some magnetic centre, falling like an arrow or a rocket confounded by gravity, compelled to face all that I seek to escape, the centre of my orbit. Perhaps it is the worn paths and tracks themselves or the contours of the ridges I turn to climb, but all bluff me, return and rebuff me in time to the scene of my crimes.

Industria, I recall the name my friend Weasel gave it: a pall of grey smoke and misery hangs over the place. Oil refinery chimneys and shipyard cranes punctuate its sky, its sordid buildings drenched in centuries of soot, its clouded windows like the misted eyes of the old or insane. Children play barefoot in its streets their obscure games, enacting in mime the brutalities of their parents, coming home drunk, picking fights with strangers, leering, jeering, eager to maim. I venture, saunter, over the weird edge where their muck and grime peters out into blighted grass, Nature shrinking from the shock and the shame. A once-cobbled lane, now patched and filled with desultory tarmac and drains. Their little faces turn, my ears burn, in less than a few minutes they've devised a new mission and enough ammunition to aim the lot at my head, stones, rocks, bricks. I'm wise to their tricks, the little pricks, unrestrained like their parents by police or morals, I pursue them each purposefully then beat them with sticks, until they cry, restored to childhood innocence again, under this reticent sky. Picking on a poor old tramp, the little demons. How can the universe stand by and permit such injustice? Well it doesn't. Limp off home, you misbegotten splots of semen.

In time I work my way down through the steeply twisting streets, the roofs like the backs of beetles and slaters, towards some kind of a town centre, from where I can see that most of the shipyard cranes are rusting now, bloating the Job Centres with their discarded workforce like lice escaping unwashed clothes thrown on a fire, a pyre. Autumn is indeed the right season right here, melancholy the correct attire. But wait, amid the neglect and degradation, is this gentrification I spy? A joy to the eye! An art gallery fresh-painted, not yet tainted by taunts and graffiti, with a red carpet rolled out to entice to these climes the lesser-spotted culture vulture awash with disposable dosh. Splosh. I've just stood in a puddle, which puzzles me since it hasn't been raining. Yet. Wet. There it is, the explanation: the gallery owner gently washing his Bentley not a metre away. His pride and joy, metallic toy to preserve the up-sized boy.

I hover at his display, posters and leaflets and there within, eyes lifting to the background, coincidence fit to rankle the gut: my brother Zenir's paintings, a dozen of them, displayed on easels, some larger chained to the walls. I push my way in, ridiculous little doorbell ringing its heart out above me. They'll just love me, an old tramp from the hills. With a look that kills, a well-manicured young lady confronts me from her desk with a sleeveless dress. Without frills, asks: *You in the right place, grandad? You forgotten your pills?*

Do you know me? —I retort, not the sort to resort to obsequity in the face of iniquity. *I'm his brother, you know, the artist's…*

Really? Her eyes and mouth widen, agape, three great orbits of rouge and kohl. *You're Ithir, his brother? Zennad Learmot is such a genius!*

Zennad? Is that what he calls himself these days? —I mutter, but she is rising from her dais in a haze of perfume and curves fit to refract the gaze and nasal cavities, a display I dare say, if I had the libido today.

She comes closer and swings her head, examining my distinguished profiles from various angles like a sculptured bust on a pedestal, and gasps: *My word! There is a striking resemblance now that you mention it! But you look pensionable, pardon me for mentioning the unmentionable, while he looks half your age.*

Not so! I protest, enjoying a long look down the front of her dress. *Indeed I am the younger of us… by about three minutes while our poor mother rested. But he has since had the benefit of the best medical care and doubtless various spurious surgical enhancements, while I have lived off fresh air. But appearances can deceive and usually do in my experience. I shall outlive him, I guarantee it, and am better in bed.*

What? You old sot, you're not right in the head. But come to think of it, he did speak highly of his brother. You don't play the...

Fiddle and whistle and piano, yes, as well as the fool.

That's it. And he said you were flippant and perverse as a rule. Rude to a fault, in fact, I recall was his phrase, and a fine one worthy of praise even among his considerable armoury of witticisms. Criticisms? But no, he'd have none of those. You were his fine little brother in all of his prose. You have his nose, distinguished as is the brow. Would you like a coffee now?

Six sugars please, I like to stock up. When do you lock up?

For lunch? Surely you're not chatting me up you old goat?

Not at all, but I can father you if you like, as opposed to fathering your children, a chore I'll leave to some other fool dominated by his biology. I prefer ecology, Nature, the birds and the bees, the things they do in bushes and trees as opposed-to to each other. I've merely wafted in here on a breeze to ask you about my brother. Where might I find him this weather?

Well, she checks her watch, an elegantly numberless number adorning her freckled wrist like an alluring garter, *If you run like leather you might catch him at the pier, he said last night that he was leaving on the next boat out of here, to Oceania, where he boasts that most of his rich clients stay, ones who can pay his exorbitant prices. We only get to exhibit them here as part of some cultural grant given by do-gooders with ants in their pants, sycophants, pedants, who think that the downtrodden poor ought to get to enjoy his work, them being his subject so often. I mean, look at this one here, The Heroic Dockworker he calls it, doesn't that have you in tears? Of sorrow or laughter we need not discuss here. And this one, The Fretful Fishwife, worrying whether her husband has been lost at sea... it makes a great diptych with The Lipsticked Whore...*

But I am gone, gone from her door, leaving her rambling like a prize-winning bore.

*

I reach the dilapidated dockside just in time to see the white ghost of a luxury yacht pulling out, and on its deck a stout lout of a man waving, misbehaving, engraving his image on my mind: surrounded by young ladies in tight leather dresses and combed-back tresses sipping from wine glasses, and I confess to feeling jealous for a few seconds. *I reckon, you know,* says a voice at my side, a total surprise, *-that bloke looks like you...*

And who may I ask are you? I clack, stepping back, *-Some cheap hack pursuing that goon for your latest titbits of news to amuse the somnambulating masses?*

He takes off his dark glasses and rubs his eyes to peer at me more closely, morosely, preparing to administer some sinister truth in insipid doses. *Police...* he says, releasing his disguise and watching my eyes widen, as he lifts an identifying pass up at an odd angle to dangle in my face. Brace yourself, Ithir, here comes the revelation. *And now can I see your identification?*

Mine? I slap my wretchedly empty pockets, eyes bulging out of my sockets. *Are you serious? Delirious? I'm a tramp, man, a vagrant, one of the silent army of the indigent, the homeless, the hopeless, the couldn't-cope-less, the financially defenceless. I don't do D.H.S.S or P.A.Y.E, just B.Y.O.B in brown paper bags, **beg**-your-own-booze, born free and keen to stay that way, any day, ever day. Anyway, the answer's no.*

So... you must have a name though?

Wilberforce Fontainbleu

You know what? He grins. I've made his day. *I don't believe you. Will you accompany me to the station please?*

To do what? I'm not chipped like a stray puppy you know, not yet anyhow. Or are you lonesome and eager for company along the way? I mean, I know it's a rough area here but it's not so bad that you couldn't make it home safely alone, you being a policeman and all.

Not at all. I relish a good fight. Physical or verbal. Your patter, like your breath, is terrible. Walk this way so I can take a sample of your DNA then be on your way. Please, after you.

Well whoopee do, police harassment to add to my fiscal embarrassment, what daring-do you people resort to when bored, instead of remedying endemic street crime and vandalism.

That's quite enough thank you, of your high-camp lip, rampant cheek to-wit, which all goes to fuel my suspicion that you're the brother of that twit Zennad Learmot. You're way too intellectual for an ineffectual bin-raker in my humble estimation, policeman plod, backbone of this nation.

I take his arm. Don't be alarmed. I'm starting to take to this man, against all my better judgement and carefully distilled prejudices against such fascists in uniform who vote Tory from birth and grow up in posh schools hurling racist abuse at Pakistani bus drivers, you know the type, usually end up in Whitehall or borstal, animal aggression and the will to power being the common focus. Locusts, a plague of them in black suits, sent to torment the rest of us who just want to get on with our lives, from schoolyard bullying to pernicious taxes, praxis, an axis of banality, foul frothing foam rising to the top of a pint of boiling piss, give them all a miss or a wide berth is my advice or shoot them like pheasants if they gain flight and attain high office. Novice, this one, maybe, not yet learned the tricks, beating immigrants with sticks and memorising tattered copies of Mein Kampf like street atlases, the pricks.

What a grubby old town as he leads me through the streets away from the docks. Like they turn back the clocks another year every Sunday. Post-industrial decline in excess, middle-aged men in string vests sitting on flea-ridden sofas, loafers, watching the box all day, behind net curtains, apt to depress the zest of youth if any grows here at doom's behest, like weeds through cracks in the pavement. Statement in itself: the success of betting shops flowering like dry rot on every corner, you're getting warmer, knocking back beer and the wife in tears as you waste your money on mirages and the jealous religion of false hopes. Not a stern god, but one laughing constantly in your face. Know your place. Sink. Without a trace.

Now a fog unwinds from the quayside, licking at our backsides with the cold snout of a deathly dog, spreading grey uncertainty in burgeoning clouds before us like a plague of vague ague, as we climb a hill until we find the station, the hornet's nest at its crest, and they usher me inside. Two at the door, and more at the desk, three-a-breast, like the old joke, even inside their inner sanctum. Let's rank them, a game to pass the time as they fill out their forms to formalise crimes with. Transgressing the norms. Oh let me be done for something outwith their normal tawdry boundaries. Four constables, two inspectors, a superintendent, an assistant inspector, an insistent prospector, persistent investigator, prospective Phil Spector impersonator, a translator of desultory street lingo, a real-time narrator, a digital recording operator, and an unplugged vibrator. Bingo. The tape is running, the questions cunning.

Photographs of some bloke on the table. *Are you able to tell us if this man is you?*

Who? Now hold on a minute, guv, this havering is the limit, innit? What's this geezer done that you want to frame an old wheezer with his misdemeanours? And unless I'm wavering, wouldn't I remember if I'd done something unsavoury?

My reasonable bobby who's called Caldwell, now hands over to a knob called Solihull whose hobby is psychology, and a medic called Prezic who probes my skull beneath the hair and finds a scar that interests him, which he rubs eagerly as a clitoris. Then they throw more photos on the desk in random array, X-rays from days gone by. They say that's me and I shot myself in the head, attempted suicide, failed like everything else I tried. *But why?* —I cry, half-believing, half-interested in this strangely familiar stranger's tale.

Jumped bail, high-tailed out of the constabulary's clutches. Last seen as a tramp on crutches. Amnesiac, just like you. And just how much do you remember of yesterday or the day before, Mister Fontainbleu or should I say Learmot? And the crunch is... he slaps the desk with his fist for effect while his friend munches biscuits. *This slime spoke in rhyme... all the damned time. How does that chime? Sounding familiar?*

Not in the slightest. How perverse. I'm strictly a blank verse man... Damn.

They all look at me accusingly, disapprovingly. Daring me to hang myself with my tongue. I'm sweating, breathing like an iron lung. *Why,* I repeat quietly, *why did this ned put a gun to his own... err... cranium?*

A crazy story, of which we believed not a single word. Caldwell chuckles as Solihull crackles his knuckles, amused by a memory flickering in his seedy cerebellum like a dodgy seventies cinema showing soft porn. *He said he'd seen into the future and seen the man who was going to run him over, and took a note of his number plate, tracked him down and invited himself over, then stove the guy's head in with a brick until it resembled raspberry pavlova. Didn't half make me sick having to peruse that scene and lose sleep afterwards, I mean he might at least have done it over the sink. I hate mess, I must confess.*

Why did you grant bail to the slime at the time, if he'd confessed to such a heinous... err... misdemeanour? I ask, sniffing inconsistency like a keen predator of a novel editor.

Nah mate, he only confessed in his suicide note, that was later, pardon me, I have conflated.

Caldwell, being a constabulary of lesser vocabulary, wrinkles his snout, thinking this explains the smell. Well, it was me, nerves loosening the bowels while I watch my vowels, but that's the least of my postponed confessions in the present session. Friction of cheeks vibrating. Symptom of the large intestine cogitating. Procrastinating defecating. Indigestible herbage of verbs not conjugating.

At any rate and in any case... Solihull sighs, tiredness in his eyes of a thousand lies given and received, deceived, the dancing veils of half truths that have clouded his ken like a Victorian opium den, *–We'll know soon enough with just a swab off the inside of your gob you old knob, saliva and all that, DNA, the old viral double spiral, Lady Godiva, naked mother lode of genetic code. We'll see if you're your brother's brother, or some other unfortunate nutter.*

They lead me to a cell to contain my smell, but I can't contain myself, I must confess, I tell them I could do with a bath and they all laugh but mine's the last: a bed for the night's a blessing not a blight for a ne'er do well. And bedded down, my wires unwound and trailing the ground, without a sound I trial the dial hidden on my chest beneath my vest and all my resplendent gowns and then I'm gone, lost and found, voyaging past and future like neighbouring towns. It's been a jail without fail for a fair while I see, place of incarceration with cruel reputation for ten generations, serving gruel to the nation's hapless reckless fools fuelled by booze and fights over floozies. Woozy, is how I feel, contemplating it all, right and wrong, fact and fiction merging under the same grey pall, like that maritime fog outside leaking under the walls. I see men in ancient attire, filthy brigands, despairing paupers on death row, footpads, painted harlots with rosy cheeks, lawyers, drunken fighters with their faces bashed up blue. And here I am observing, from behind iron bars, but more free than any of them dislocated as I am from time and space, behind my dreaming face.

How much time goes by? Day and night merges in the dim cell's half-light, and I voyage into the future too, see that the jail will be demolished soon, pulled down by vengeful bulldozers under the duress of some edict of progress, and a park replace it, my word, resplendent greenery to make a sap complacent, and a monument to commemorate some poor sod who they murder in custody. Justice, conscience, regret expressed in rhapsody. Wonders will never lapse, nor sins to require forgiveness. And in this, I see I am but a minor player. A soothsayer who came this way, went hither and thither, old sot condemned to live then be forgot forever.

I wake at last, into a mighty hunger, bleary and confused and thinking I am younger until I see my chipped nails and ageing suntanned hands, remembering some random fragments of the lands that I have voyaged through, the many faces and voices surrounding me in momentary cacophony, a symphony of prosody without remedy, dissonance and assonance resolving into a dance of chance dissolving to the here and now and anyhow. I wipe my brow to wish away memory and the sweats of night fevers. Fugitive escapee from my self who hides in traces of every life except his own, that which I would disown as long as I am loaned some other mask and task to call my own.

So before I wake too far, let us make use of the magical power that flowers in the twilight of the waking brain. I reach out my hands and part the iron bars inside my eyes as one would some minor irritations, swatting flies, bending walls and space about my face and ears. Reality tears, thin as gossamer, pliable with suitable mental pliers and shears. He who sleeps steps outside of time, and when returning but by habit discards the hazy power he has lazily acquired to make seconds out of years, and more: as some mighty blacksmith to bend all reality to his will, to call halt to events and re-forge their mettle, making courage out of fears. Pop, slop, burp, slurp, I find myself outside my cell, ready to check-out of my hotel in hell. And there smiling is my reception: a plethora of police dumfounded by my deception.

Sitting and poring over reports and analysis, read-outs and print-outs, contemplating and cogitating to the point of black-outs, reaching for white-out, unable to think out how I have circumvented their designs on me. Solihull, Caldwell and Prezic, and several more in tiers, ten-a-breast in black like crows in rows in repose upon the branches of a tree. All looking not at me, but at a screen and a sheet and what it all means: *Wilberforce Fontainbleu, you are free to go.*

How so? You mean to say I am not the brother of that lauded and applauded piss-artist after all?

A shaking and scratching of multiple heads. *We don't know what it means, Einstein, except that our data is in error and we need to pull in Learmot himself again. When he gave his own sample, he must have been pulling our ample chains something obscene. If you see him abroad in your begging routines then tell him we need to pick his brains and saliva again. Until then, let's forget the whole stooshie and keep it schtum between men. You still here? Do we have to tell you again?*

So there you have it. Turfed out of a fine hostelry without even a bacon butty to initiate the day, no overtures of apology audible to propitiate my indignation per se. I wander in the fine light rain the same grey streets again, but feel lighter of foot and of brain this time, washed clean of grime and dizzy in the drizzle which urges me forward to some route and pattern whose puzzle remains beyond my conscious grasp. Until as the sun comes out at last, I find myself in a kind of city square and plant my arse on the first clean bench I find there to let myself dry off in clouds of steam rising into the sun's beams and I close my eyes, seeking after fond encounter again with the recently lost land of dreams. Distant sound of thunder, my hunger shaking me, making me delirious, but nothing serious, I am content to savour the free effects of an entirely legal high, and gaze up occasionally, through flickering lids, at the mothering blue sky.

And now who do you think passes by? But that glamorous lassie, a snooty sight for glad eyes, that I so recently engaged in idle conversation in her gallery by and bye. Striding across the square, not on her venerable vulnerable own of course but with her complete toss of a fashionable boss togged up likewise in co-ordinated designer drag of expensive price tag and fetishised name and all that game. Shame, he'll probably spoil the quality of our intercourse perforce of his premade preconceptions of my social station. No matter, nothing ventured, nothing for breakfast. I break my silence, and the two spin around, expecting violence perhaps, not just from me but from the various other unemployed now newly standing on corners emerging from the shadows after the recent rain. I fancy that the bloke even fingers a flick-knife in his inside pocket (glimmering above ermine satin lining) and am impressed that his dress stretches to such practical lengths. Tense, until I wave my hand, and the lady recognises me at last and laughs, recalling what a jovial fellow I am, what flowing words spout from between my yellow teeth, and gives a decent hearing to my latest verbal scam.

I have misjudged both him and her. For within a jiff they have me seated in some mid-price canteen with a plate of steaming victuals in front of me and I try not to slurp too much while they pick at their cold salad greens, puzzling at what my every cryptic word means, tossed out between mouthfuls of bacon and sausage, potato scone, black pudding and beans.

Are you really Zennad Learmot's brother? —the bloke, called Pieter enquires.

Shoosh, I say, *not really, or to be precise, on this issue I am now entirely confused. The police in whose custody I have just finished languishing for days, convinced me that to say so would be a very bad thing, he being a bad bloke. But then, dispelling my fears, their scientific tests by which they put much stall, have firmly convinced them that I could not under any circumstances be Ithir Learmot at all.*

And what do you think? —asks the girl, earnestly, called Cassy, *Who do you think you are?*

I am uncertain, truth be stated. But some of what they related to me of Ithir disturbed me greatly, rang more than a comfortable number of uncomfortable bells. But tell you what, though my stomach swells I'm still not sated, any chance you could get the waitress to have this plateful reinstated?

Waitress! —Pieter shouts with the unexpected confidence of a streetwise lout, attracting the ire of others seated roundabout. *Sounds like you have amnesia, my friend. Did you bump your head or over-imbibe paint stripper as a nipper or at some point in the recent past by any chance?*

I know not, but sense and suspect that Zennad Learmot knows some useful fragments of this cryptic plot. I'd swear he waved at me from his yacht shortly after last we three met, a salutation more respectful I wager than he often reserves for just a down-and-out old sot watching from the quayside.

He recognised his own likeness you mean? —His semblance, your resemblance?

Or his sibling... troubling, trembling. No trifling matter, when your twin is mad as a hatter, an escapee from the loony bin. Rifling through his grey matter to find a way to put a quick distance between me and him.

Not so! —Cassy exclaims, strange triumph in her eyes, *For in a few days he has another exhibition in a rival gallery already rallying an audience, sworn rivals of our good selves, a few miles west of here. He kept this one quiet, but it sounds like a riot.*

I devoutly thought west of here held nothing but water, Davy Jones' Locker, my memory retains no name for there but Neptune's domain, excuse me if it ought to...

Ahh, then you've not been in Industria long, friend, or your memory loss is more extensive than my hair loss... Pieter laughs good naturedly, *for these steep streets and antiquated quays are but the ancient and smaller part of a vast diaspora of mud flats around the cliffs from here, which stretch out towards the setting sun, where great ships are still built and welder's torches burn.*

Here, Cassy says, fishing in her pocket to retrieve a writhing glossy fish, a leaflet, one of just three left, of boastful superlatives and other advertising pish, declaring Zennad the greatest contemporary painter of his age, nay, a sage of visual prophecy to topple the current mediocracy, to coin a well-aimed phrase I bet they wish they'd thought of, but they're not half as good as me, hooligan of neologisms wasted on the begging trade. A tirade of brag, interspersed with photographs of two paintings and one of his self-important face, an expression I long devoutly to replace. *At the Anchor Gallery at nineteen hundred hours in shirts and ties, canapés, vol-au-vents, petit fours, crap crêpes and hors d'oeuvres will be served.*

The man's a wanker. From this firm conviction I will not be swerved. But too much rancour's apt to disturb the stomach at this early hour, so let's leave the knave inside his ivory tower of the mind where we can find him later, the great masturbator. Coffee arrives and I contrive to smile, swallow back my bile and share small talk with my kind benefactors who ask me questions dazzled by my bohemian lifestyle:

Oh how can it be that you escape employment and attain enjoyment consistently, constantly, so fancy-free?

Come, come, don't look so glum, you talk out of your bum surely, I reek like a lum and kip in tips, sipping nips of industrial-strength booze. Surely that's no ruse to outwit the glittering lifestyle of gurus such as you? I pay a price to escape the vice of wealth which makes you slaves, measured in my dirty fingers and malnourished gums. Your fears are only phantoms of humiliation and diminution, mere mental irritations, while mine are the urgent peril of whether I shall eat or starve, find a dry bed or writhe in rheumatic damp and chill. My vocation has the power to kill, while yours just to break your will. And there's the irony perhaps, the grain of wisdom in your effete longing after what heroics you hallucinate in my wretched state. My will is honed and validated daily by the indomitable deathly power it opposes, while yours languishes, soft, unkempt, amid a bed of roses.

We salute you, Ithir, or whatever name you wish to take, for sharing with us your morning break. Your eloquence with words makes all our verbosity seem dull and brown as turds. Fear not on account of your unwashed status. To you we open our hearts and close our noses. It is a triumph of our will to pay this bill and your departure saddens us at the prospect of a long hiatus without your wisdom, your warming air, your cerebral conflatus.

So it's done. I shake hands and wave my goodbye thanks. That girl's revealing dress is surely fuel for half a dozen wanks, should my memory and strength be willing now the flesh be weak. Streets open up before me, and my hand grips a little sketch Cassy and Pieter drew me, to guide me to the Industria docks. Overhead, flocks of geese fly south and the few trees I pass throw leaves down at me like lover's notes. All orange and gold colours, the wind turning cold, autumn murmurs and whispers everywhere, building its insistent insidious argument towards a mighty declamation of wind and fog and rain, a veritable roar to settle up the score with spring and summer.

I walk and walk again until the narrow streets drive me round the bend, quite literally and viscerally, as passing around the base of a headland I am at last released and unleashed into a broader vista. *Hey mister!* –Croaks a nearby voice and I am amazed that anyone believes I possess the wealth of choice to throw them coppers. Then I realise, tears in my eyes of gratitude, that my breakfast hosts have gifted me a new jacket from off their shoulders, making me look bolder and with attitude, perhaps the means and latitude to attend tomorrow's vernissage, that's a Private View, to me and you.

What a vast landscape unfolds before me now, of rusty girdered cranes, of rails and trains, of flat scattered bodies of water stretching to the sea-filled horizon, where steel and iron clang and stammer as ships are built up from scaffold. Tiny figures flicking to and fro, lit orange and red by the frequent glow of oxyacetylene torch and glancing hammer blow. I walk on for hours into the heart of it, the heat and beat of it, passing clanking goods trains and old canals whose cobbled walkways slither hither and thither with moss, the cries growing louder of men at work shouting one to the other from derricks and gantries and gangways and wheelhouses, edifices of riveted steel plates surging and curving, towering and glowering around me and over me.

A relict, a prelate, old derelict entering a derelict sector, with a predilection for good diction and prediction, I rest at last, on an old rusting capstan still twined with frayed ropes and threadbare hopes and consult my makeshift map, a folded square of tat, not much to guide me or make sense of where I'm at. My fingers trace the ink lines like vines eagerly searching for bowers to bear fruit, when a near voice sounds at my oxter, making me jump like a toaster: *Are you lost or in doubt, doubting Thomas as I make you out?*

What? I spin and turn about, giddy as sin, fractious, anxious not to let this intimate voice raid the sanctum of my cerebrum, hectoring like plankton unstoppably microscopically vectored to in-swim. *What did you call me?* I find myself facing an old hag, whether bag lady, destitute or prostitute or inmate of an institute I dare not hasten resolutely to avow.

Thomas! –She laughs with open mouth and gaps in blackened teeth, an exotic dancer of the heath no doubt by moonlight when nowt's about, a witch I mean, clean off her trolley, old dolly with no lolly, dressed in rags. She takes my hand in hers and starts to read it like a book, lifeline, deathline, every clammy cleft and fissure, cranny, crimp and nook. I look around, expecting to spy her pimp then finding none turn to contemplate her fanny, and my cock which needs a sook. But no, that thought's all rotten, misbegotten and as sordid as the actions such sordid words denote. Christ, for all I can tell, she might be a bloke, a tranny. Best play canny. *My name's not Thomas, madam, you are sore mistook.*

Bollocks, Thomas, quit babbling like a brook. I knew you straight off from a distance as I saw you recently in a dream. You are ancient and reincarnate, come by this way again to test the ways of wayward men.

Come again? Queen of rubbish, you dazzle me with your compendium of impudence, your hot air hotter than the synchronised flatulence of ten fat men.

Ah! Haha! How sweet to hear your vile entreaties of abuse break loose again!

Again? Again? I beg you please don't take advantage of my intermittent amnesia. I entreat you, if it please you, I beseech you, to leave that topic well alone and tell me only truthfully if we've ever met before.

Not in this life, then, if answer that I must. But trust me, take it as a primer from one old timer to another, brother, you are True Thomas The Rhymer.

Confused, upright, twisting to go and escape her entwining arms like ivy, these last words make me pause strangely instead, as if I were dead and she picking wildflowers from my grave. All energy leaves me for a second and I slump back down and she takes a place beside me and we both fall still, gazing outwards to the wave-frosted seas and distant trees. Years pass over me, blowing fleetingly, as migrating birds and the sun-dappled tides of falling leaves, shadows of clouds that have passed over centuries of days. And for a second, I lose my place in the order of things, then grasp it more deeply, as a beach shelving steeply at my feet gives way to depths too dark and out of reach to contemplate without barbiturates. Who am I really? Or any of us, when these momentary faces, customary pleasantries, as curtains: time takes and pulls away? The thought makes me dizzy, as if the ground of all the world were not land at all, but sudden-turned to glassy ocean smoothed flat by some chill and unfamiliar hand, mirrors on which I dare not walk for fear that like ice they'd crack and let me fall.

I remember so little... I say quietly at last. *And supposing this the case, what purpose can it serve that man should live and live again?*

The witch takes my hand and smiles a small flicker of solace on her lips like the first flame on dried tinder. *Live well, is the only answer to that ancient riddle, press on and trust that the great prize before us is great indeed, and who could doubt that who looks about and sees the wonder of creation? What task and goal except a glorious one could summon up such power and invention, mobilise so much beauty and organisation to its cause? Only a fool would hope to meet God. Better to tremble at the thought of being in the presence of such genius and savagery, judging by the evidence he leaves around us. It is enough to be part of it, joy enough and terror enough.*

Terror? Savagery?

As the eagle tears out the heart of the dove, as the playing child drowns in a summer riptide, the swollen river plummets over misting cliffs, stars explode and galaxies collide. The scale is too vast to support significance or hierarchy. No conscience could sanction it, nor strong man bear its load.

You are as mad as I am, clearly. I sigh, *shall we go?*

Where, dare I know? The witch laughs, *just where does your little map lead I wonder, heaven, purgatory or that other place below?*

Nothing so grand, I say, unfolding it again from my hand. *To an art gallery where my scoundrel brother is said to be scheduled to appear, tomorrow or the next day. My name really is not Thomas by the way, but you can call me anything you wish and regale me further with your tales although I think them wind and pish, while we amble there together. One need not be erudite, to see that you are no urbanite with the packed diary of a socialite, but indigent and desolate and rather lonely and eager for respite, a condition I can understand, as well I might. What name shall I call you by?*

Mary... she says quietly, falling in at my side to match my stride. *Scary Mary to the local youths who uncouthly abuse me for my toothless looks. Fools dodging schools, they should all go read books if they want to escape this hellish nook, instead of honing the skills of torturers.* Evening is coming on now, and the rain which has held off the last hour or so out of decency, is now rearing up to strike in sunset clouds of purple, black and blue. A breeze lifts and I fancy we shall be soaked as seals in another mile or two.

Och, tut tut, they're only children... I sigh, *they often hassle me too, my solemn advice would be to kill some of them with bricks, if I were you.*

She chortles and we enter some dingy streets of partially inhabited façades, some by ivy and moss and weeds, others by people with glowing lamps and window frames. Cobbles beneath our feet are ruptured and fissured with green veins of decay, that like panicking fever seem ever about to overwhelm the eye and win the day. *Who was this Thomas then? Some ancient figure, some hero of yesterday?*

You do not know the fairy stories, the children's rhymes? But if you have forgotten even your own childhood that need not be such a surprise I suppose. He lived eight centuries ago, a writer, a soothsayer who predicted many things. Future battles, the deaths of kings, that London will sink beneath the waves. People said that the fairies gave him his powers in return for the dangerous condition that he must never tell a lie, and neither did he until the day he... I nearly said died. But of course they say he never died, he simply went away one day, abandoned the castle where he lived, when the fairies sent him a sign.

What sign? And what on earth were fairies anyway? – Things so ludicrous that they've packed their bags and fled our world because educated people are no longer able to contain such nonsense in their heads?

Ahh... Scary Mary laughs an old dry croak. *As if the capacity of human heads for nonsense were in any way limited, as if they haven't established that with gusto over recent history. Fairies will be aliens now, and ghosts or something else in centuries hence. You protest too much! You're fooling no one! Tell me honestly, that you have never seen into the future or witnessed passing legions of the dead, felt the very ground shaking where they tread. Tell me that, as you plead anonymous, then I will believe that you are not True Thomas.*

The rain has come on now, in huge fat drops, and Mary leads by the arm through some ruined doorway into the shell of a church, the interior piled high with the rubble of its own demise. Like the scene of a sacking or bombing in some chapter of history which must have passed me by. *Here, I hide here often,* she says, *when the rain is heavy or the tide is high, my bread unleavened or the end is nigh.*

We walk into the centre of this dismal stage set, surrounded by high ghostly shards of ecclesiastic vault and groin disassembling in the grey mist of rain. *What? You talk in riddles...* I whisper as she ushers me through a ragged entrance into a cave of piled rubble at the centre of all this, and kneeling down beside her as we kiss, she puts a hand inside my shirt, caressing my nipples until she finds… the dial, and cries out, whether in delight or fright I can't decide.

'Tis just like my dream, She wonders wide-eyed in the half-dark, *and the wires too trailed down your sleeve. Oh do not leave tonight but stay and show me pictures of the worlds that you have viewed through your strange device. Show me the future of mankind freed of sin and vice. Show me nobility and hope, there's a nice boy, now.*

This is no toy, you silly cow. If I show you your own future, your death, have you any idea how that would send you potty? And the future of humankind, like its past, is one fraught with pointless slaughter. If you were my daughter, I would strike you blind before I would annihilate your mind and brain with the strain of what you'd find there.

Aha! Scary Mary chuckles, placing her old claw hand around my whitened knuckles. *So now at last we find an answer, a reason for your loss of recollection. You are a victim it seems of your own contraption. You could not bear the burden of the future any better than I, hence this suture.* Her fingers have found the wound on the back of my head, the same one the police found so stimulating. Irritating. *And is amnesia so bad?* She croons more softly. *It was the greatest prize, the Greeks and Romans believed, given to the good at the end of their virtuous lives beyond the fields of Elysium. Wisdom in that you see. Forgetfulness meaning death and birth, is the price we pay for immortality.*

And yet, only recollection can be our salvation, our waking up. I sit upright, spurred on by a new realisation. I must wake up and remember. We must all wake up and see ourselves in time, as the watchful head of some great multi-bodied creature rousing, rising from the slime of millennia of grime and crime. But Mary has her hands on my shoulder dragging me down and slumber comes heavy, dancing on my twitching eyelids and the aching in my rheumatic cracking bones, contracting sinews and muscles. No need for tussle, just give in, sleep is no sin but the beginning of all healing and erudition, an appointment with the divine intermission, quenching of ephemeral ambition. The music of rain invades my brain in a grand serenade, a parade of fading images falling as leaves from trees, see-sawing and gnawing on the breeze, fleeing all light and sound approaching the ground, and longing, longing for the shade.

Woken the next day, the air has been washed fresh by the torrents from heaven. I poke my head out of my bomb-crater midden and enjoy the new sun on my face and my place beneath the soaring blue sky. And asking the perennial question 'who am I?' this time there are suddenly fragments of answers, jigsaw pieces, shards and slivers tumbling in. I struggle to hold them all at bay, all out of order, a house of cards, ill-fated, images of murder, mayhem and dismay. I killed someone once, an innocent man. The contraption on my chest was once connected to some larger apparatus of which I was master. The power overthrew my reason, made me commit treason against the natural scheme of things, bringing... bringing, all this long slow disastrous season. I clutch an autumn leaf in my hand, borne to me magically by an obliging wind. Yellow, red, pink at the edges, like the burned paper of sheets I once held in my hand, destroying instructions on how to create the monster that I am. The fall of man is as the fall of God, trying to forget his own power, seeking hopelessly some hiding place, some bower in Eden beneath which to bury the memory of a deed. Clang, clang, The Big Bang. The bell tolls for thee. The black dog of guilt will dig it all up, no fear, sooner or later, there will be tears.

In gratitude for the dubious favour of a glimmer of self-knowledge, I turn my dial as I gaze at the sky and tell Mary what I see there, hearing her murmur and wake and take my hand. *High above where only aeroplanes traverse the sky, there will in future be canals made of glass or some other material or miracle we lack the current words to grasp. I see what look like slow boats moving in these arteries, although their speeds must in truth be fast, our whole atmosphere one vast net of these conduits converging at vertical roots which dangle from the clouds down to hubs where people wait to be fired up like grapeshot or seed. No war and disagreement only this glorious aerial interconnection as the canals and folds of some ethereal brain...*

But what? She is strangely silent, and disengaging my wires from the stones in which they have entwined all night I find that a shaft of slanting morning light has penetrated our den to illuminate a state of things beyond my ken. I see now to my dismay that she is only bones. A skull, femur, tibia, claw of hands clutching faded old fabric shawl wrapped around her. Some fragments of hair still blowing in the air, white as thread, one of the dead, a victim of whatever horror once happened here. War refugees fleeing to a sanctuary which proved fleeting. I hear the bleating of the last cries of their children, then tears in my eyes, cover my ears, tear at the dial on my chest and stand to leave, swaying, bereaved and grieving for the invisible years like glass through which I have unwittingly peered. My friend cannot help me any longer, nor I help her or ever change her fate, and alone again as ever, I must go on.

Wounded, haunted, hunted by all the emotion that I flee, I limp again onto the road, my heart sagging from its load of human sentiment and hope. My little map still guides me. As I walk west again along the canalside paths, I find one road rises rapidly and the more I follow it, climbing, I get out of breath, until looking back I can see the waterways below me and the ruined church some way off behind. The hill rises higher still as I go on, until I reach the end of its irrational and unexpected topography. I stand at the edge of a cliff, the ramp to the apex of a vast slag heap of shale from where I ogle at the scale of everything around me, astounding me: the shipyards and the furnaces. The blue sky above growing pale again already, shrouding all too soon in the pall of hazy smoke from all this toil and spoil. Curling waterways surround me as the coils of some vast serpent within whose constricting embrace I am embroiled. A dead end, no easy way back down to ground, I retrace my steps a little then flounder, sliding down some dusty rampart like a refuse chute, vanishing in clouds that choke my lungs, until at the long-awaited bottom, I stand up shaking, emerging like a clown, caked white from head to foot with pink holes for startled eyes, a pretty sight to dazzle passers by.

A passing crowd of dockyard workers in blue overalls applaud me as a variety act, a stray minstrel from an impromptu daytime cabaret, and I pick up a nearby bucket to use as a makeshift bowler hat then take my bow. I grapple in my pockets, my ash-appropriated apparel, looking for my map again, and everybody laughs, thinking this mime is timed for them. I carefully unfold my crock of gold and sit down to interrogate its treasure: some measure of meaning to these streets which delude my feet in ongoing displeasure. There it is, ex marks the spot: Anchor Gallery, emporium of jewellery and fine contemporary painting apt to produce audible awe in educated men and in ladies fits of fainting. *Corner of Admiralty Avenue and Tobago Wynd,* a voice says not unkindly, head leaning over my shoulder, *you'll get there if you follow this street west for three more miles.* He smiles, helping me up. *I've just finished my shift, could give you a lift that way, if you don't mind sitting in the back of the truck, seeing as you currently so closely resemble three cubic feet of walking muck.*

So I do. So what. A bit of luck at last. Thank fuck.

Jump up. What's up then? He shouts over his shoulder as he drives, as if such a mode of conversation is normal where he comes from, communicating from astride steel beams a hundred feet apart. *What is this lark then? What brings you to these parts and what draws you to an appointment with the arts? You don't look like the pretentious type I have to say, more the kind for a pie and a pint washed down with some vigorous swearing and a manly game of darts and several loud ingratiating farts.*

Nonsense, I laugh, *appearances can be deceptive and human beings seldom selective or receptive I find to those whose characters run contrary to all the stereotypes they keep constantly in mind. As you'll be gathering any minute now, I have the vocabulary of an educated genius and the verbal wherewithal to deploy it any time and place with reckless haste any old how. Silly old cow!* I shout aloud to a wobbling hobbling old woman my chauffeur has just narrowly missed mowing down, so sideswiped and blindsided is he by my dazzling diction and grammatical know-how. *In summary, I may look like a down-and-out, but in fact I am an intellectual lout, unplugged and disconnected from all the usual rules of etiquette, more inclined to cross my eyes and dot my teas than watch my peas and queues. A ruse, you see, this disguise, to misdirect the eyes, do you not surmise?*

Bloomin eck, mate, you're a flaming nutter, I don't want no trouble mind, I've got no quibble with your kind. I'll just drop you off at the next available corner where you can reacquaint yourself with the gutter. Sorry, but I like to run a decent law-abiding lorry. Just pose as a ball of dirt again and the next refuse van comes by might take you to a quarry.

No matter, I retort as a last resort, *truth be told I was already growing weary of your patter. It would have been football next then doubtless your unsavoury views on immigration, how to save free kicks and this drowning nation by enlistment in The Front, The League, and stave off inundation by the barbarian delegation. Frankly I'm proud to be mad, black or queer, or whatever hallucinated terror you mistake me for in error, to get me out of here. What's dirtier, my face or your mind? And what place shall I find more of my kind? Not this planet, and not this time. The verbally flamboyant were long since deported, out of sight and out of mind.*

No matter indeed, for I surmise my trusty map has failed me not, and my destination requires a walk of just one more block. *Thar she blows,* the Anchor Gallery, an establishment redolent of outlandish blandishments, manned already I see through its glowing window display, by a regiment of anal artisanal aficionados, connoisseurs, poseurs and raconteurs. *Mine's a glass of Chardonnay, what's yours?* All Armani suits and champagne flutes, silly shirts and giggling flirts. Laughter in bacchanalian baritones and soprano semi-quavers. Oh do come in, don't stand there, don't waver, don't dither, come forth, come hither. A drooping banner all aquiver, substantial signage to declare that Zennad Learmot is here, there and everywhere, with even a photo of his veritable visage to fix passers-by with his studiedly difficult and complicated stare, those brooding eyes to vex and hex and sex and hypnotise. Strong spirits on hand to retrieve the swooning from the land of sighs.

I'm looking all about to find my brother, like a wolf in the henhouse sniffing out the greatest concentrations of fluttering feathers, I find instead the gallery owners who introduce themselves as Eustace and Polly, he somewhat feminine in lace silk curtains, she somewhat macho in braces and Doc Martens, a gender juxtaposition I ponder abstractedly while I help myself to nachos. Their own dress so laissez-faire that they seem to take my sartorial degradation as symptomatic of a new one-man movement of vagrant street art with attitude and court me for a platitude on the painting of the great Zennad. I am unable to resist, while flicking olives with my wrist and other tricks like firing cocktail sticks across the room, to resume my interior monologue, externalised temporarily for the masses, on the subject of my sibling, whilst endeavouring to knock back several wineglasses without dribbling.

Learmot, I would say, in his infinite resistance to definitive definition, is loath to give ammunition to the crass critic and the avid admirer alike, by riding on a trike across the paint-splattered canvas of his reputation with a few careless words tossed over the dyke. Of course I'm mixing metaphors, splitting infinitives, and quoting clichés like there's no tomorrow, but it would be a matter of sorrow were the man to unmuddy the waters of his complex allegories and thereby to stand naked before you, so it falls to pseuds like me to do it for him. I'd say his work is lewd, crude, food for thought of a kind best served as antipasti rather than a main, which is to say it is not altogether plain nor altogether good nor wholesome, indeed at times it's rather nasty. Take this one here for instance... I wave my hand and part the retinue, leaving me feeling somewhat lonesome as I continue, *I'd say that in this one he has nothing at all to say, but passed a day contriving a whimsical puzzle to keep your muddled brains at bay. But while he may be glib and taciturn, recalcitrant and intransigent, I though apparently indigent, have much to say to him... and come to think about it, I've come all this way to cross swords with the master. Where is he hiding amongst you, the bastard?*

But... but... says Polly, unable to restrain her giggling as if my lecture has been an entertaining interlude of folly and whimsy instead of my burning of the widespread flimsy drapes of blindness, a kindness that I'm only slightly tipsy. *You've just missed him. He breezed out an hour ago to return to his ship for a good night's kip before ploughing the ocean's waves in coming days. His autumn tour advances as the seasons of the year. Oceania beckons, so up and off he must be out of here.*

No! I clench my fist and buttocks, close to tears. *He eludes me again, this could go on for years. Can you tell me where the brigand moors his frigate, rests his vessel, parks his barque, corrals his coracle?*

What do you think, oracle? –Eustace leers laconically. *The nearest pier to wherever he can bank his anchor, just like parking a motor car, ironically, which is to say: not far, basically. Nine hundred yards straight out that door ajar past the whisky warehouse and the Fishermen's Mission.*

Don't be a wanker. No need for rancour regards my stupidity at which you're hinting. Thank you. There now follows a short interlude of sprinting.

*

I find Zennad's yacht down at the dilapidated dockside without too much trouble. As if contained in a bubble I slither my way on board past his bodyguards using a subtle mixture of blackmail threats and physical violence. Met with silence. They're black-suited gangsters' men who Zennad likes to surround himself with for reasons of glamour, clamour, carefully releasing spurious stories to the press every six months about how their bosses are threatening to kill him for unpaid debts and bets. These play almost as well to the adulating millions as his invented mental health issues, stories of which I find particularly offensive, given that I am, in the current parlance, *the real deal* in that regard. I have read Zennad's stories in newspapers I've pulled from bins, wrapped my feet in and stashed under my head as pillows for my cardboard bed. I fell hard after my diagnosis with schizophrenia, I seem to have been remembering recently. But whether before or after my botched attempts at self-trepanning and putting a bullet through my head, I am more hazy on.

I reach his cabin and it seems confusingly empty until I turn and face its full-length mirror, and I see him there disguised as a tramp. *Still rhyming all the time, brother? —He drolls. Come to treat me to some couplets and sonnets in Iambic Pentameter, have you? Or is all this claptrap rap? Chap chap* (he taps his head in the age-old gesture) *Just what part of the brain did you mess with to start all that stuff up? Pass over that cup, and I'll pour you a brandy. Handy, a drinks cabinet cabin, wouldn't you say?*

Just dandy. I sit down at his elaborate antique table and he joins me.

And the time travelling, he sniggers, *how's that going? You still got the wires down your sleeve and the dial on your chest? Where you been to recently? Thirteenth century France or the Yucatan meteor strike?*

I can only go where people were, I tell him quietly, gritting my teeth. *There were no people around in the time of the dinosaurs. I told you, it's like hypnotic regression, past lives. I can go back down the chain of births and deaths, but only so far.*

And forward? Zennad laughs, indulging me, not believing a word, the turd. *You've been to the future too, right? That's what you told me last time, that night…*

I nod, slowly and silently, starting to shake violently, little splashes of brandy spilling down my sleeve like blood.

And that's when you really dropped the ball I recall. Just what could you see there, dude?

The w-w-worst thing imaginable… I stutter and splutter into a spasmodic cough, rough, hoarse.

Ahh, I see… your own death I suppose. Hardly a surprise, we've all got to go you know. He grabs a Turkish rug from an ebony chest and wraps it around my shoulders to warm me up and stop my shivering and leads me over to the cabin window, from where we both look out at the sea, the patterns of waves, opalescent, transcendent, nascent.

No… I manage, pulling myself together, sipping the drink, trying to remember, trying to think. *That was the first time, I should have left it at that. But I took matters into my own hands, killed the man who was going to drive the van that ran me over. Would have run me over. Tenses, damn, so hard.*

Which is why you always talk in the present tense now I suppose, as well as rhyme, no crime, one word's as good as another. But murder, are you serious, brother? And why tell me now anyhow?

Murder's the least of it. Causality, casualty. The future changed, I changed it. The world ended. Will end... if I don't die, didn't die as planned. The butterfly's wings, changing things with each tiny beat of its tiny wings.

Hence the gun, and the bullet through the head. Zennad nods sagely now, accepting, philosophically. *It's a pity you botched it really, isn't it, sunshine?*

Did I? Or am I, perhaps, I sometimes wonder, are we, could we be, already dead?

It's always there as an existential possibility, granted, he muses, eyes to the ceiling, *–even without resort to amateur ballistics and supernatural statistics. But you're a whacko, Ither, out of your box, brother, we both know that as well as we knew our own mother. And while we're on weird thoughts, here's another: what is a twin sibling anyhow but the ultimate, organic, personified rhyme?*

I'm nodding back at him, agreeing, lifting my eyes, and he's reaching out his hands to embrace my shoulders as I lift mine, to his neck. An embrace, he thinks, but his face now, stunned, chokes, turning slowly blue as I throttle and throttle. Horrible sounds of diphthong and glottal. He catches the bottle, the brandy with his flailing hand, I duck, luck, and it lands against the mirror. Shiver, shuddering of a whole world cast asunder. Thunder. Silver light forever, all tumbling down to the ground, the fragments resounding, surrounding, astounding. Turn around to the glittering sea and run, run like a river.

The thugs let me out without a whisper. Just another one of Zennad's eccentric excursions, down the gangplank and out to the dirty-black town. Maybe he goes out some nights as a woman, a master of disguises. No prizes for guessing how he gets his kicks and inspiration, undressing all the repressed with his eyes, as he passes them, wearing dark glasses. Sizing them up for a canvas. From the hull, one particularly dull-witted henchman hails me: *Still sailing tonight boss?* No loss, the loss of my brother. But it hadn't crossed my mind that I could steal his identity. Heaven sent, if I meant to. If I wanted to.

*

So the plan is laid, and slept on seems almost sane. Soaked by overnight rain and kip in a skip placed next to a drain, I court sympathy at the rear door of a charity shop with my best puppy eyes and emerge some moments later with a whole new attire: smart jacket and trousers not quite completely ill-fitting and a fresh shirt and tie only torn and stained in places hidden from the eye. I stroll back to the Anchor Gallery with growing confidence in every gliding stride, borne up and inspired by my sartorial magnificence to impending acts of verbal munificence, eloquence and sleight-of-hand too quick for the eye or the ear or whatever orifice one's audience cares to bring to bear. People turn and stare as I pass, an ass come back as a messiah. A liar? But True Thomas would fail at any such endeavour. Therefore some deeper truth must here be being divined, I devoutly opine. I vow to sever any links with my recent past, and emerge resplendent, should anybody ask, not as Ithir but as Zennad, artist and entrepreneur, and catching a glimpse of myself in a passing shop window, pause and decide to go in there where they shall cut short my hair.

Have you had any holidays yet? −Asks the charming young lady who shampoos my head, along with penetrating questions like*: Have you always had a beard?* In return I regale her with verbal virtuosity for ten minutes as she crops my wig into the debris around my chair, portraying myself with such skill as a freewheeling divorcee millionaire that she is too much in a tiz to respond as I whiz out the door without paying at the conclusion of the procedure. Such behaviour is permissible for sheep, and I forego her steep rates in the hope that she may choose to weave my famous and wealthy plaits into something useful to stave off the winter for a family of three. Now I am free, and several grammes if not a kilogramme lighter. Next time I'll invite her to my luxury yacht on the seven seas.

And so I breeze into the gallery disguised as my brother and announce my intention to follow my recent sell-out exhibition with another. Aghast, Polly and Eustace smother me with kisses while I grasp their asses, both of them so as not to be deemed sexist, or should an unknown observer exist and insist to my face; as if I've just misplaced my glasses. It's off to the adjoining studio at once with sleeves rolled up and canvases stretched like groaning victims on the rack, and Polly dashing out to buy more paint waving and winking saying she'll just be right back. Eustace collapses in a chair and smokes a Gauloise in a state of heady ecstasy as I unfold my troubled psyche in a frenzy onto the easel in front of me. Surprising myself as to how much I remember of all the faces and places I've seen in recent days: I watch them all emerge transfigured, transplanted, revealed in different ways for the hidden spirit within them peeled like fruit then pealed out like bells, announcing their taste, their texture, their sound and smells. Belles, beaus and portmanteaus at work, in action and in sweet repose, all the panoply of human kind engaged in financial monopoly, enrichment, enslavement, or decline. I pluck it, crush it, and distil it into wine.

But look, this can't be me this thing, these graceful curves and skilful lines so unrehearsed but just right each time. The colours sing. It's as if I'm just a twit, a conduit, for some force unearthly or divine brought to earth through the lightning rod of my current state of possession, obsession. The paint moves as if it is blood from my very veins, the canvas flexes like human flesh, beating, responding to the touch in a way too familiar. I lean a finished canvas on a pillar, and start straight off upon another then another. Damn that brother of mine, this stuff is easy, occult transgression, allowing demons intercession. I'll teach the twat a timely lesson.

This new work, Eustace groans with hand to temple, *it's the best yet, vigorous and tempestuous, in fact I may be getting an erection.*

No problem, I say sportingly over my shoulder, *the toilet's just over there and I'll hold the fort while you give that some attention.* Tension, pent up for weeks it seems in my body like a spring, is easing now in this flood of inspiration and the consolation that it brings. *I didn't know I could even paint, where do these skills come from?* –I find myself whispering just as Polly returns and in shame my cheek burns.

Astounding, astounding... she pouts, *that in these bouts you seem so returned to a naked beginning, devoid of self-belief and giving birth to yourself again, phoenix-like from the ashes.* She bats her lashes, and I contemplate the stash of cash they'll give me when I've lashed fifteen of these fuckers to the mast. What a blast.

But now you ask... I say, *are you telling me I've expressed sentiments like this before?*

Oh yes, she says, impressed, *every time as if you've forgotten all ability, and reeling in incredulity at your own pictorial virtuosity. Just as Rilke said about remaining an eternal beginner, or Ernst said of a painter never finding himself, as Picasso said of how painting must regain the eyes of innocence, or Blake of course who thought himself a fake dictated to by intercourse with an angel with unusual forehead muscles...and what was that other quote... from that bloke in the bowler hat from Brussels?*

I stand back and survey my own efforts and see dockworkers straining shoulders and the curving hulls of ships all knitted into quips of colour and lines entwined like cosmic decoration, a constellation of human labour forged into a visual broach, encroaching... I find my head swimming and my legs growing weak until with the slightest tweak I am tumbling and gone over like the Tower of Babel, unable to resist gravity's insistence, dropping my sable, hitting my head off the corner of a table...

I wake sweetly cradled between Polly's bobbing breasts while Eustace takes off my socks to massage my feet in some misremembered fragment of First-Aid, bringing my eyes to tears, releasing smelling salts from beneath my seasoned socks which could put him out for years, when calling out an ambulance would be less of a performance, a paramedic less of a headache. Have I only been out for seconds? The telephone is ringing and when Eustace goes to get it I get a sinking feeling reconstructing the tirade I soon surmise his ear is getting. What a pity when I was enjoying such a rest between Miss Polly's breasts, now starting pitching, heaving, as a mighty galleon setting out on stormy seas. The man on the other end of that phone, you see it seems, is me, in a manner of speaking. And Eustace's voice is squeaking now, useless to explain the contrary information leaking, inundating his overloading brain. But how can this be? I thought I'd smothered my brother or put him in intensive care, at least partially succeeded in getting him out my hair. Not fair, not fair.

Oh misery. I am unaware how he has pulled off this latest escapologist's mystery, the logistics of mesmerising mist by which he has wriggled out of such a twist, Houdini-like eluding my grasping angry fist. But clearly the time has come, dear brother, for one magic trick to be mirrored by another. It's up and away, with a leap and a push and shove, still staggering, out through the first window I can get to without a set to, and into the thrilling freedom that I love. Sprinting down the street with my clothes still dripping with paint like blood on a murderer's mitts, racing like steeplechasing, running like the shits. Warehouses and street after street speed by me, breathless I look back, expecting pursuers to defy me. I race towards the quayside, spotting the sails of that blackguard's ship but what's this? His boat is sailing off, and on the bridge I see some shady figure wrapped in blankets resembling he, with a telephone to his ear and waving fondly, fondly ridiculing me. Desperate, I glance about and untie some unlikely skiff to jump aboard and before I've thought things even half-way through I'm rowing and floating, boating while Zennad's gloating, sailing out into the blue. And by the time I weigh the oars exhausted, an hour hence, I'm nowhere, drifting out into the estuary, pulled by mysterious tides, along for the ride, nowhere to hide from the sun up above or all the storms to come. But at least the land is lost behind me and my pursuers overcome. Whatever. Whatever I have done is done.

~

PART

THREE

Oceania

Mesmerising mist. Sparkling diadems that twist as I open and re-open my eyes, writhing on the boat floor. Grilled like a prime steak by the inescapable sun for days. Amazing. Blazing haze. Burns. Then it turns. The autumn chill and winter storms. The doldrums gone. The punishment begins, for crime unspecified. Puny plaything that I am in the Gods' hands. Did I really think they'd grant me free passage to distant lands? –with all this water to enact my slaughter? Too good a chance to miss, this hiss and roar of spume and piss. A chance to show a wretch how to retch, a full how to be empty, to starve and die of thirst. Women and Ithir first. Abandon ship, I think not. No strength left for anything but lie in state, rigid as a twig on a river in spate, staring up at my creators' big sky to ponder why, and quietly, quietly cry. Lose consciousness with any luck and stay out, all spun about but safe within my spiralling mind, falling down through sheets and sheets of dreams, gleaming reams, uncovering, discovering, sniffing like a bloodhound the deeper secrets out. Leave the world behind to find a kinder place with slower pace and fairer face and... grace, grace. I brace myself to meet my maker, or Nature both creator and annihilator absolute and resolute in the crash and clash of atoms, recycling of minuscule molecules. My farewell is heard tell. The old destitute is dissolute.

Or is he? Dizzy certainly, when the storm subsides, and too weak to reason out the vagaries of tides and the cause of that strange rocking motion against the sides. The ocean? The notion comes at last, with the keening cry of a seagull swooping to survey a potential fresh repast, that I have not yet breathed my last, but struck dry land, lodged hard and fast. I grapple and topple, the hull tipping to spew me out onto the sand, served on a fine salad of seaweed. I crawl an inch then a couple of feet, then collapse again, my defeat complete, deep, deep into a deeper sleep.

The slopes are steep of the sandy place I slither to, hitherto unvisited where I meet an old man humming to himself as he takes apart machinery on a workbench in his glass conservatory, except that what's outside is not suburbia but an endless desert which encroaches, poaches, apocalyptic, on the edges of his once-green domain: a few last potted plants as vestiges and bastions against the coming end. I sense that he is my friend, though he never looks up as he goes on working, but finally says: *Ah, welcome, I'm so glad you came, again.*

Again? Come again? I ask, but he continues resolutely with his task until I ask him what he's at, at which he quietly laughs then says: *Building and repairing the clockwork hearts of men.* At this a tiny clock beside him on the bench explodes into activity and sound, its sudden hour of alarm come around, at which in one short and effortless motion, he hoists a mallet and smashes it down without even a frown, destroying it completely into a mess of crushed gears all smashed and strewn around. With a sense of uneasy threat, I find myself drifting as he goes on working, sifting, shifting, being pulled back away by some intruding voice, until at last by gravity more than choice I am awakened again, back into the world of men.

I am in a hospital bed, not dead at all it seems but small, examined as a microbe under a microscope by a plethora of physicians adorned with stethoscopes, peering at me with their thick spectacles like submariners through the windows of a bathysphere. Stuff this, get me out of here. A flood of tears, I am forcibly restrained firstly by strong hands and rubber bands then by pain and swollen glands. Baring of the arm and priming syringe, cringe, impinging on my liberty and dignity. Fight and kick. The needle's prick. Doing their duty to sleeping beauty. Sigh. The morphine hurtles in, eyelids drooping, groggy, foggy, useless, lousy, drowsy as sin. Diving under, I blunder with a sense of wonder through a blue kingdom where seals and dolphins swim. Until led through a door on the ocean floor I am no more. And so reborn, begin.

Eyes open, bright daylight stinging. My ears bringing the sound of the sea, somewhere nearby through glass. I look down and see I am in a wheelchair and panicking, tear the tartan blanket aside and grapple and massage until I can decide with pride and relief that I have not been amputated by some over-zealous thief in surgeon's gown, just taking it easy in my queasy wheezy state is all, it seems, has been intended, I can ease my frown. I call out and soon have the furniture upended, expecting some expectant nurse or worse to come and have me apprehended, but there instead appears a middle-aged woman, looking offended. *You are awake at last, Mister Nithna, how marvellous, I must go tell Horace of your progress, he'll be speechless with joy and restless with questions your attention to employ. Oh boy oh boy!*

Questions? Never mind yours. They can keep for a year or two for all I care, but I sure have a few, I can tell you. Horace?

Doctor Horace Stockbridge, my husband. Director of the Institute.

And Nithnawhat-the-hell did you call me?

Nithna, you said it was your name each time you were asked.

Under considerable sedation and hallucination I would wager, and with my mouth scarcely any further open than my ass. Am I out of danger? You're pretty thorough with a stranger. You'd think I was your brother, not a clapped-out old tramp. I feel like a scamp, a dog in the manger, sitting here in the splendour of this mansion, and not out on the streets. I look about, my eyes popping out.

But we don't have any streets here, Nithna. You are in Oceania now, the region of islands got about by boats, but... she puts a hand to her throat. *My word, that is one of our first clues to who you are and where you have come from. I must get Horace before I blow this.* She flees in glee through the door.

Know this... I whisper to myself, turning the wheels of my chair with inexperienced grasp until I find my reflection in a full-length mirror in a gilded frame, where I am shocked at my emaciation and battered complexion. *Nithna is not my name, but nor was Ithir, or whatever one I had before that. I flow like a river forever, never quite putting down roots, in cahoots with no man and no place. My face, my face!* I grapple with my unexpectedly clipped nails to unclip my human mask, a task, a trick that never fails, but I flail, hearing footsteps returning, my ears burning, I reach up for my hair and nothing is there, or everything rather. Getting in a lather. No electrodes and network, no wig for the scalp lubricated with talc, but the real bloody thing. How long have

I been out? Long tresses from functional follicles. Bollocks. My hands leap to my chest and part my vest. Rest. As you were. They nearly had me there, choking, strangling. The dial is still fused to my flesh, some wires left dangling.

Mister Nithna, may I introduce myself at last? His huge broad hand closes around mine and crushes it as would a falling pine tree. I remember his face vaguely from the gallery of scoundrels in gowns who went to town on my premature autopsy. *What a blast to see you awake and partaking of the art of conversation leaving my wife Emily aghast. You'll be eager for your first repast, if you're able. I'll wheel you to our dinner table.*

Wheel me? Stone me, that's a lonely homily for an old bum and prize pedestrian to hear or bear. It would do me in to be without me pins. How long before I can stand on my own and get out this chair? And what about my hair? My wig, you dig? Where have you put my neural net, my electromagnetic scalp nexus? –The whole shipment. Connected usually to these flexes, thence to my chest and my trans-temporal equipment?

Woah there! Slow down, our honoured guest, he says wheeling me with extra zest lest I slither off, *we've much to ask you about that strange contraption on your chest. It had all our best people vexed. We're quite convinced that it's completely useless but separating it from your rib cage is quite another matter. Seems it's fused at a molecular level to the bone, stiff as iron, hard as stone.*

Of course it is, you meddling pratt. How else to be sure of where I'm at in time and space? My neural net, can you go and get it yet? I need it, must I bleeding plead it?

Let it go. Relax, I implore you. We have carefully kept all of your clothes and personal effects aside, everything the tide brought in with you, Nithna. Our scientists and journalists have had quite a scrap trying to decipher your spurious retinue of crap. I do recall some rusty wires in a curious grid stretched across your lid, but whatever the thingamajig did it won't do now unless your can renovate and reconfigure it somehow. Jiggered, kaput, kapow. Capeesh? You'll walk again in less than three weeks from now, isn't that the more important answer that you seek?

Meat. A whole plate of it before me. Soon the conversation starts to bore me compared to the simple joy of rediscovering the task for which I must my teeth employ. Glorious taste and nutrition, mastication without inhibition. Placation of the fundamental drive to stay alive. Eventually I look up with a start to see that Horace and Emily have been watching me gorging in a state of both primal horror and incipient quasi-parental pride. Confused, I fart, and soon am offered apple tart. My eyes adjust to the view from the patio doors before me: of a beautiful beach reaching out to the hissing sea which so recently released me, and for a moment *She* seems like an entity, an empress fraught with enmity that resents my recent egress without her consent. She often has that murderous bent, although today I notice over my pastry lattice that she is serene and calmly balmy. I have escaped her army of white horses by some oversight or insight, heaven sent.

Balmy? Am I Barmy? After sweet and repeated biscuits and cheese, rendering me replete, the patio doors are drawn aside to introduce me to the sea breeze and I clutch the tartan blanket to my knees, fit to freeze. My god, the seasons have changed while I've been away in the land of nod, snow and ice cannot be that far off. They push my wheels across the soft fine sand, and guide me with a gentle hand to gaze upon this whole new land: Oceania, a thousand islands of disparate size and dispersed population, stretching randomly to the horizon. And at this moment, mooring, disembarking at their private jetty, I see a uniformed steward with two wards, jumping juveniles no less, explosive charges one might attest. *The children are home early!* Emily exclaims with joy, and bounding up the beach they come to inspect me as their new exotic toy. Psychotic boy and neurotic girl, they soon have me in a twirl with my stomach lurching, with all the respect due to an ice cream lolly they spin me like a supermarket trolley, but soon repent this immature folly, sent off to bed and a sound birching. At rest again and thankful for the refreshing breeze, I throw my guts up on my knees, thankful for the thoughtful blanket, thinking if I had a child like that I'd spank it.

Later in the study over coffee, Emily lights a roaring fire and I reflect on how I could get used to such a life, notwithstanding the recent strife with the nippers, whom Horace assures me are usually nice as chicken dippers, and smiling at that odd simile I wonder if they just need more battering, but keep that last to myself, the concept somewhat less than flattering to one's hosts with whom one toasts a new beginning. *So tell us now, Nithna,* Doctor Horace sighs, rubbing his hands as to receive a prize, *commence tonight and proceed as you see fit over coming days, to tell us all that you remember of how you got here and who you were before. Open the door of memories and dispel the haze.*

Now, here's a rum conundrum. I remember plenty that will make me sound mental. Like angling to strangle and smother my own brother, or trying to disrupt his exhibitions and impersonate his style. And that's just the recent mile of a journey out of deeper darkness. What he's really harking after is the function of my apparatus, dances with the dead and flirtation with the silent nation of those to come. None of which he will believe at any rate, and conclude my sorry state is ripe for the asylum, which by the looks of this domain will doubtless be on another dedicated island. Deny him that whim, I'd say. I who cannot swim. Trim, trim the truth, True Thomas The Rhymer. Desist to resist. Offer no violence. Prefer, and proffer: silence.

It seems that what I lack, casting my mind back, is most of my recent narrative. Thus pleads this plaintive plaintiff. *Perhaps I was mugged and thugged and drugged, flung into that boat in which you found me. I believe I was in Industria, but it's all a blur of grey confusion and effluvia, as if some trauma to the head leaving me for dead has voided my retention, not to mention some mental bruise, a psychiatric ruse in play to keep my prying poking fingers away from some terrible contusion, a confusion of the id and ego, ergo I best not try too soon to lift that rock and risk the shock of being mobbed by the clacking callipers of a hundred nightmare crabs giving me the screaming abdabs.*

Goodness gracious. Such self-lucidity and perspicacity, not to say violently vivid vocabulary. Industria is certainly a rough old locality. It wouldn't surprise me to surmise a couple of ne'er do wells felled you there for your cash with a quick swipe of a knife with scant regard as to your life.

Perhaps you were a man of means whose wife and weans are even now scanning the news each day with bated breath for confirmation of your death?

I take a deep breath. I can see why my supposed name proposes me lame at this sort of game. Truth is more easy than lying, as living is than dying. So soon, like a goon, one is in hell and frying merrily. Verily, tell what is true, and you'll come through. Affirm firmly, and quit denying. *I know not, for I remember naught for sure of who and what I am and whence I came. I have fragments of childhood recollections, and perhaps if I share those with you, starting at the beginning as it were, in time you might accrue a clue or two as to who I am and what to do.*

Please... says Horace, lighting his pipe and stretching back in his upholstered sofa and kicking off his loafers with a grin. *Begin...*

One of my earliest vignettes is of my mother leaning over the sink and peeling spuds in a little red tub which I later found out was a peculiar invention the like of which I've not seen since... called a potato peeler, with sandpaper on its base and a little handle to the side with which to commit potato frittricide...

Fratricide? How very Freudian, almost as if you are avoiding...

No, frittricide, as in potato fritters. It is a joke sir, of an unfunny but linguistically inventive kind. Lame, as it were, a joke in a wheelchair. Oh yes and here's another: soap suds by the hundreds, and my little feet drumming in a green bathtub, and a dream I had of this afterwards in which a world war one biplane fell from the sky and smashed through the frosted glass of our bathroom window and the pilot had a white moustache which seemed to be made of the same white soap suds like fluffy clouds, and I can still hear the loud sound of his propeller blades spinning and recall my terror at his aeronautic error and see his goggles all misted over like the frosted window glass frighteningly shattered. I remembered all this for years although it scarcely mattered. One of my earliest dreams or nightmares I suppose, first evidence of creativity composed in my repose.

Fascinating. Horace strokes his beard. *You notice the importance of colours in these memories and dreams? First the red then the green and the white. Colours are like flavours to a very young child in a way that we forget as we get older, immured by constant stimuli of the eye and the neural cortex. Red is the most exciting and appealing, green somehow atmospheric and wistful, but within each nuance of the spectrum a thousand other stories and suggestions are waiting to be detected. This is the basis for our response for instance to oil paintings in later life.*

By Jove, you're right. Because come to think of it, my next early memory is of a curving country lane with a bank of blood-red poppies in the hedgerow by its side. And my brother and father are up ahead, waiting on me because I am so small and slow. And I see that they are walking towards a dark green pine forest at the top of the road, into which I know they will turn and go. Then later that same night we are woken by a leak in the roof in heavy rain, and I am in the kitchen where I see the same red colour: this time in the plastic of the bucket placed beneath the dripping water from a hole in the ceiling. And I remember a smell: dry rot, pungent. But where the hell was all this? I cannot tell. But you're quite correct, that pale blood-like red has a particular quality quite unlike the security of rich post-box crimson or the gay allure of violet and pink. But what's the point of all this analysis do you think?

Everything. We have established that you were not an orphan for instance, but had a mother and a father and it seems a brother. Just one, or could there have been another? And on and on the evening goes until I nod off half way through a sentence and drift into repose in my clothes I suppose.

*

The next morning, my hosts are wakened with a grand surprise. Having noticed their study furnished with various stringed instruments, I open its glazed doors and roll through and after a minute or two have a viola tuned and am administering a sweet reprise as morning medicine to anyone who cares, bringing down the stairs the apparition of an enchanted Emily barefoot in her chemise. I play on, letting the leaves of trees dance in the breeze outside as if in balletic mimetic enactment of my melody, pathetic and affecting in its aesthetic, redolent of the indolent melancholy of angels, pitying humanity to the edge of tears. The years roll over me, music easing as a balm and bringing calm, dismissing fears. Whoever and whatever I am, can rise above this tawdry mortal slot, discard our lot, and offer up a psalm to our unknown creator. Birdsong, word song. No greater honour than holding and unfolding beauty's banner in this manner, high above the bleak plain of pain's domain, enjoying momentary sunshine before the grey onslaught of rain.

What was that tune? Emily, now joined by Horace, gasps.

But alas, it was mere improvisation, evocation of my current placement in the here and now. They show me sheet music and it's all Greek to me. Too much a knave for stave and clef. I know how to play in key it seems, but not to replay parrot fashion other people's dreams, only my own.

Here, take this instrument on loan. Play and play some more, we'll teach you how to read and write a score, become a virtuous virtuoso affettuoso.

But no, I smile, *I'll improvise again every once and a while if I may, tomorrow and today, but nothing more rigorous I implore you. It would only bore me. Just ignore me if I sound like an ignoramus talking out his anus, but such is the unanimous magnanimous verdict of my corpus and my animus. I need to take it easy or I feel queasy. Call me pusillanimous if you must, or take it on trust.* Motes of dust fall through the morning air as their amazed faces calculate what to make of this florid protestation. Mouths agape, fit to throw in a grape or two.

But you must have learned or been taught such skills of hand and ear, then here we have a clue to be sure of your former life, and must hold it dear. We'll recover your memory yet, before you leave here. I have taken the liberty of sending copies of your fingerprints and X-rays and DNA to a colleague in Switzerland and expect to hear back from him soon. If you've been in the hands of doctors or police anywhere then there's a chance we'll learn some more of who you were before.

Snore... I decide to mimic sudden narcolepsy to get me out of future fixes like this. Brain damage can play all sorts of tricks. Strangely, the subterfuge is no gimmick and I find I'm out for fifteen minutes. Woken abruptly by the offspring breezing in with a barrage of ululation, which brings me to a late and unexpected realisation: that they are two too young for parents such as these. Then I hear Emily warning that she'll tell the girl's mother if she doesn't behave and cease to tease her brother, and I have my answer. *They are your grandchildren...* I observe aloud, as one swerves to avoid the flying dropkick of another.

Indeed, and a blessing though they are, Emily smiles sweetly, *it is a sadness that their mother cannot be with them during the week, while she works several hours away from here in Urbis. Turbulent economic times such as these dictate such crimes in these climes, where one must make sacrifices to earn even a crust. If their father could just have lived, one might forgive our vindictive creator for this sorry state of affairs.*

Tut, tut, Emily! Horace splutters. *Must we thus bring God into our utterances? –And not keep our lamentation on a scientific foundation?*

What befell their father? I ask and touching Emily's hand for a second receive the transmission of what it takes her tongue somewhat longer to unfold: *He drowned in a boat capsized, was lost at sea, and so you see there is a certain symmetry in your coming to us, washed up as you were like a dead man on our beach, bereft of identity and speech. It is as if...*

Tut, tut... again old Horace shakes his head at his wife's irrational intuition tantamount to treason, at odds with his own medical mission to shed the light of mathematical reason upon the sea and land.

...As if by God's own hand He sought to return to us a message manifest in man, as a test from above of our love and capacity for faith. And if we could but embrace this stranger, so too will He guard over the soul of the lost and

drowned one. The children's father you see, was our only son.

Tears fill my eyes and hers, instantly. *I am so sorry for your loss. The death of he who was your child is a terrible cross to bear, and yet... and yet we must rejoice that he leaves two children of his own so fair.* My hands and Emily's pile over each other like the vaults of a little cathedral wherein votive candles flicker, honouring the hope she gropes for, which I know to be alive: that we do not die, but fly to a place which no eye can spy, nearer than a heartbeat, more distant than the sky.

And Robert, our son, you see, he played the piano and the violin, and though we've tried to get the children to take lessons, you are the first person to truly bring those sweet instruments to life since last we saw his beloved face. Truly, it is God's grace that has guided you to this place, from wherever it is that you have come.

I am humbled, madam, and a little afraid, of the importance you attach to my appearance at this moment in your life's parade, but suffice to say though I am not your son nor any spokesman for the divine one in which you believe, I can offer you news of the afterlife for such is a place that I visit daily in my dreams and visions, and I shall pray for your son.

You are a psychic? A priest? A monk? I see her spirits rise, in her widening eyes.

A mystic and a seer I fear, of just the kind that your good husband would seek to debunk. But I'll say no more on this for now, lest I darken your brow or his and cloud your domestic bliss with an issue that I see divides you.

Emily opens her mouth as if to protest this perverse cessation of verse, but Horace interjects with the converse: *Quite wise, quite so, Nithna, let's let it go, all this to and fro on the dubious subject of the human soul. Whether its dissolution is absolute or relative I cannot know, but that the living must concern themselves with life, you, I and my wife can agree, despite our recent blow. Come, play the piano for us and inspire us and the choirs of angels that crowd our invisible environs for all I know.*

And struggling to approach the pianoforte stool, I note the boy dressed now in his best and ready for his lift to school, is no fool, but has been taking note as if to learn by rote, from the doorframe's edge, all that we have said on the subject of his father's demise and cannot disguise his curiosity.

*

Next morning, apt as a warning, I find Horace Stockbridge's daily copy of the Oceania Advertiser lying before my eyes on a silver tea tray by the porch. And there on the front page is a reference to an article inside on the artistic mage of our age, Dirze Learmot. Who? My brother so it seems, is of as nomadic nomenclature as my mature self, perennial, evergreen and eager to be seen. And there he is on the Arts pages, espousing the delousing of our effectively infection-inflected age with the wisdom of a sage, or a charlatan more like. A harlot and a tyke, with paintbrush in hand, leading his devoted acolytes like deluded Carmelites and Canaanites, ammonites, dripping like stalactites, sanctimonious and trite, as the Pied Piper in full flight, off to his nowhere lair. Who cares? What is this ire I feel rising in my gorge, ere I spy his visage and his daily dressage? What dread deed does this anger feed? What event does this bent of mine presage? But wait. Satisfaction comes late to those who wait. The news is that a scandal brews, added as an unauthorised addendum to this piece, the wily weary reader to amuse. Rumours of booze and loose morals on his boatly cruises of late. Oh cruel fate. A bruise, a stain upon his reputation. An accusation, made by some as yet unnamed woman, disavowed and disabused, pregnant and indignant, cast off by the upstart artistic toff as easily as he weighs anchor. Queasily, the approbating public weighs its rancour, dries its powder, loathe to loose its outraged arrows until the approaching reports grow louder, erring on the side of charity, awaiting clarity. Ironically, for just a minute I feel sympathy for the scoundrel. As if the lives of the great judgemental 'they' are any better, or would be, if they but had the opportunity to have their gossamer morality tested pell-mell. Given a free run in hell I'm sure most of them would have my brother bested. But mellowly they dwell in their suburban purgatories of sanitised sanitary ware and air-freshener smells.

What is it attracts you in that story? –Doctor Horace asks over my shoulder, looking older from his night's sleep pushing Sisyphean boulders up blue remembered hills in heaven or hell he cannot tell without the right equipment.

Deportment. In a word, it does not seem quite seemly or sporting how this famous man conducts himself in public.

Quite so, Horace agrees with a hearty grimace, *it's enough to make you vote for a new republic, communist utopia or such like, wherein such cavorting shrikes could not impale their shite on the tree of life all day and night. But do you like his paintings? –Surely this is the real issue, which even he has forgotten in the sodden haze and misbegotten blaze of his name's fame. It's all a game, but at its heart there's still a puck flicking to and fro.*

Fucked if I know, I sigh. *There's something there, or was once, but now it's just an endless echo of itself, to produce more produce for the shelf. The man excavates himself but is a quarry long since scooped, no longer serving marble but exquisitely marbled poop.*

Guffaw, guffaw, old Horace holds his sides and yawns his maw, *You have a wicked way with words as he with turds. Come let us try our exercises for the day. Firstly, on the beach, to walk a few yards on sticks with your unaccustomed legs and loafers, then afterwards with all those memories out of reach in the comfort of my study and my sofa.* And though I'm eager to stand upright again, less like a wheelbarrow and more like the sons of men, I am less enamoured with the glamour of uncovering my past to order, some of it best left over the border in no man's land out of the reach of prying hands.

*

Reading alone some of Horace's weighty tomes in his leviathan of a reliable library, the little angel Annabel saunters in on snow-white feet to whisper in my ear that her brother Nigel says I am a witch who can talk to the spirit of her father. To which I reply I'd really rather not attempt such intimate communication with a relative of theirs so dear, for fear of causing upset and dismay.

What!? Her eyes flash, as her grandmother shouts on her to get ready for bed. *You commune with the dead in the domain where the dead's laws hold sway and yet refuse us news of those we love. Are you a raven or a dove? Just with whom are you hand-in-glove? –The devil or the one above?*

Look, I say, and lift a candle by its brass chalice handle, *Let us watch the falling wax as it spills across this page, revealing the words of the dead and secrets of the ages…*

I'll tell! I'll tell! Squeals Annabel. *–Tell Grandpa how you desecrate his books!*

No you won't I wager, when you take a look at what the hot wax spells. And sure enough, the white spots congealing reveal by what they conceal a different text plucked at random from page 113 of Horace's original 1903 edition of Erskine Childers' The Riddle Of The Sands, as follows:-

Solitudes of sand, ephemeral shallow sea, deeper arteries surround the great convolutions as it were the veins, tide throbbing, infest our fine days by daylight manifest an innocent stranger verify our true course new excitements not in any danger at all, stranded in a spot the constantly recurring question this time we were.

And this from page 204:

Enough! I shall never in reality shudder for our self-invited guests with puffing risen for a demon of that unearthly light, they stood like delinquents at judgement passively to accept morning on return finding a shore meant for his friend, anxious little vessel come so far drinks pleasure alone of three since the fog cleared.

But what does it mean? –Annabel leans in, eyes wide, intrigued.

You saw me pluck the book at random from these shelves, did you not? And yet it speaks eloquently of my life and your father's death, as stars set within the same system, linked in some strange way that none of us can yet know. It tells you not to be afraid, but to go on seeking answers as to the true nature of life and death, to revel in the mist of the mystery of the voyage of life, with all the breath we have left. Now off to bed. And banish all this nonsense from your head.

That was my father's book. Look, at the front pages where he's signed it, see? –Are her last parting words to me before she scuttles away, yielding to her grandmother's pleading. And after she is gone, the candle burning low, I take the old book and press it to my brow and from this fragment forge a voyage through time towards their hapless father, Robert. I see him twist in black space, his face distorting in the last rigours of drowning, then his body rising and falling with the distant tides carrying him far from all the living, forgiving in their kissing motion of nourishment and dissolution.

Closing my eyes and lifting a pen from the table, I let his spirit enter into the husk of my body for a minute and write a message rapidly in the opening leafs, beneath his own signature. And when I revive with a shudder I read there the words of another, but written in the same distinct handwriting:

Dearest Bell and Jell, weep not for whom the bell tolls,

but as the wave rolls, move on and love,

content with the consent of your dad who smiles above...

A door clicks behind me, and I catch a vanishing glimpse of little Nigel withdrawing to his granny's calling.

*

Idling in the study in the evening late, tuning a violin a thought occurs to me as to how to re-animate my contraption which my host has been subtly and persistently recalcitrant in providing me with electrical wires for. I shall take up the playing of vigorous and violent traditional reels, get the whole house dancing and in the midst of their squeals break a string with a little razor blade most cunningly concealed. It's either that or take the cabling from their lights and heating, which would in winter be somewhat self-defeating and ill-befitting a guest so pressed to the breast of his gracious benefactors. Laughter, sounds of delight from a distant room… the children's mother come home, not a moment too soon, good-timing. I'll have the whole brood miming my scheme as a team. The miracle of music, none can refuse it.

Then Mrs Stockbridge swoops in and I lose it. The tune, the melody of life. My strings sag. I view by osmosis for a moment, by a dead man's eyes, this woman as my late wife. And in truth, though I am often over in business in the darkened lands on some supernatural enterprise or another, it hits me hard for once the waste, the bitter taste that death leaves in the mouth of life. She is beautiful and lonely and so lost to him who so comforted her until recently. And who could approach such a monument to love as she-without-he, without defiling such grace indecently? Presently I recover my composure, plastering over my emotional exposure.

You must be the mysterious Nithna, Horace's prize patient and guest dilettante savant and clairvoyant fiddler. My little angels Nigel and Annabel have been telling me about your secret sideline as a medium. I am Gladys, pleased to meet you.

I take her hand and shake it, shaking a little that she already knows what her children have disclosed of my supposed powers. And there over her shoulder, old Horace appears and glowers. I see the thought flowers in his head that he has let something unwholesome and unnatural into his erstwhile rational nest, that a weed has seeded in his bed. To boot, can't get that thought out of his head once it's taken root. Thinks I'll fill a swag bag with loot as soon as my pins are operational, and be for the off, having ripped off a toff. Sensational. Not to be scoffed at, such a scenario, but I avoid criminality as a rule, being conscious of the penalty in this life and the next. Nonetheless, I shan't vex myself with the complex hex of people's expectations born of their prejudices, just content myself with avoiding the constabulary and the judiciary.

And so, dear lady, well met. I shan't impart tidings of your dear departed yet, but weave the riddle of my fiddle music's sound to gather all your wounded family round for an innocent evening of reunion and celebration. See the little ones' feet dance in among their elders as saplings in the forest yearning for, turning towards, the light. Upwards, onwards, wisdom lives in rhythm as the deeper language our bodies speak to our creator, even as our minds sleep, intoxicated by exertion, making this assertion: that life is good among good company, as trees among a wood.

So true to my plan, as often as I can and tact permits, I let the occasional string let rip, with a zing and a whip, accompanied by a witty quip, and quick, quick, Horace hurries to find me a replacement each time, which I untwine and tauten up, slipping around the keys to appease the waiting dancers. And so Nithna: chancer, necromancer, secretes the broken strings, the wires he needs in his back pocket, to earth himself to the unearthly socket on his chest then so to lift as a bird with wind under its wings and joy in its breast. It will take a while, each methodical theft, fabricating a yarn on a loom all warp and weft, just as walking each day on the sand leans more on right then left, soon to recover all of what I have been bereft. Right, left. Right, left.

*

Next Doctor Horace Stockbridge calls me to his office to offer this: that he has received a letter from his esteemed colleague in Switzerland who in turn has found another man: one Doctor Erno Schwitzer, who claims to know my true identity, indeed that he handled my peculiar case two decades ago. *Schwitzer says that your real name is Thomas Leermouth, a former physician struck off for your unauthorised experiments on patients, involving hypnotic regression and electrical currents applied to the brain. Some of your subjects were damaged or went mad and you went on the run with a gun after some kind of procedure you performed upon yourself went wrong. A reward was offered for your arrest dead or alive, and the former of the two you took it upon yourself to do but botched it with a bottle of scotch and a Luger point two two. He has sent me fingerprints and photographs and here's the laugh: they do look quite a bit like you. So now tell me, Mister Nithna, washed-up brain-washed stranger, what are we to do?*

Fuck. Stuck like a rat in a hole. And another sudden resort to narcolepsy would be too obvious, though more relief than I can tell. And what do you know, but snow at last begins to fall at this moment, visible in gliding sliding parachutes of white, through the window behind the good doctor's shoulders, white as his white hair, like a hit-squad of divine mercy falling to cover up my shite. How like ballerina's dresses and the swinging tresses of lovely girls all this cascade and swirl of crystallising ice. Snowdrops falling, how very nice. Suffice to say, I think it rather lovely in an abstract way, compared to my predicament today. *I have heard similar accusations and suggestions before, all folk lore put about by louts, what a bore, I seem to recall being tested for my prints and spittle by policemen who found little to confirm their theories and much to make them scratch their neurologically-challenged heads. That Leermouth man is doubtless dead, while I, as you can see, between you and me, am very much alive. You may contrive to test my blood and saliva and all that jive and pish, if you wish. But I promise you this: when I am fully well, soon I trust, I will be on my way and leave you alone, as leave I must.*

But Nithna, my dear boy! I wouldn't dream of such escapology and all-for-bugger-all-ogy. My studies of your neurology are scarcely started. I'd be broken-hearted if we parted at this early stage. And these accusations seem to be rousing further buried recollections, the browsing of which I would recommend we undertake as a matter of urgency. Your memory could be undergoing a resurgency!

You have been too kind to an old tramp in a bind, sir, and I would be better gone and out of sight and mind, away from your good family and good people of their kind.

The doctor continues to be horrified at my convincing concoctions and confabulations. *Why are you talking like this so suddenly, Nithna? What's caused this catastrophic loss of self-respect and self-esteem? Have we been paying enough attention to your dreams? What repressed and sublimated and re-directed guilt from your past is this we're witnessing? Surely it merits harnessing for several months of study?* My god, the old fuddy-duddy shames me with his goodness and credulity. *I haven't told you yet of my latest proposal: to rid you of that foul excrescence on your chest which you hide beneath your vest. Remove it lest it fester and turn septic. Doubtless put there by some jester or cynic to delude you that you're psychic. Why, I could perform the procedure on you in my very own clinic!*

You are a sceptic then, as to my supernatural abilities? He nods his head like a buoy bobbing to infinity on the grey concrete sea of confirmed modernity and rational certainty, strapped into his sinking boat unable to admit to himself what he can plainly find: that I, and others of my kind, can float. *These accusations... tell me for my information, where is it that these events are said to have transpired? —Here, Switzerland, Swaziland, Timbuktu or Buenos Aires?*

Sylvia, the south-easterly suburb of Urbis, due east of here. He nods.

Well now that's queer. Because I have the strongest feeling that's where I'll be heading after here. Having read that Dirze, until recently Zennad alias Zenir, is eastwards-bound to escape the hounds of the press whose smiles he's found less toothless than desired recently, indeed ruthless, having acquired bad breath and a latent inclination to harry him to death.

*

And so the scene is set, the stage prepared, for me to get myself out of their hair, the noble family in whose care my recuperation has progressed so well. —So nearly ready to throw away my crutches and slip silently from their tender clutches. Last time I tried I nearly fell, but the fallen snow as night arrives gives me my final jigsaw piece for quick release. The estuary of Oceania is fresh water and apt to freeze. Imagine that, a thousand islands in a sea of ice, myriad mirror fragments in which to fish for glimpses of my true identity. Oddity on an odyssey to divine my provenance and heredity. A rarity, a man without a name, without temerity. May God judge him and his dim life without light, its hopeless brevity, without severity.

The candlesticks are filled and lit, the curtains drawn tonight as Stockbridge's island sits frozen fast in its sea of glass, and Emily and Gladys conspire against the patriarch to permit the one-night only indulgence of a séance. A joke, a party game, so harmless a distraction indeed that the children are to be invited, the whole family united, with Nithna as the stand-in for its missing piece: tragic drowned Robert whose photographic portrait adorns the mantelpiece. I hear his lost soul tapping at the backdoor of my brain, anxious for release, contact, communication. Meanwhile an hour before: I hide myself in my room to weave my violin strings into the tresses of my hair, placing a tight skull-cap borrowed from Horace over all to bind the contacts to my scalp, then connect all the wires to my chest-dial. None shall suspect. My curious headgear giving me the appearance of an elderly Jew, all orthodox and kosher, a mystic, a magician priest. Quite a to-do. Oh what a hullabaloo will follow when I show them what I can do.

I emerge from my quarters and make my way to their drawing room which I enter with suitably dramatic flourish and the flickering of guttering candle flame. The tall red velvet curtains are closed, the room disposed to melancholy and expectation. I wheel myself to my place, legs slotting beneath the table as if for a moment I am a necessary accessory to family life rather than an abomination who courts damnation with his divinations. *Hearken unto darkness, my dear gathered friends...* I begin, connecting by the wires in my cuffs to the stone of the old cottage walls behind me. *I shall be the conduit for the evening. For you I shall entrance and enchant myself, placing my soul suspended where all the voices of the night can find me. – Bind me to their lost spirits as the drowned grapple for ropes and wreckage of the life they remember. It was September I see, when Robert's boat floundered... an autumn storm snapped their mast... There was another on board with him, one James... James... Je*

Jefferson, Jim Jefferson... his friend and pilot... Gladys prompts, and I see a restraining hand cross the table to discipline her, old Horace suspicious of cold-calling, the appalling exploitation of grieving he has read of in his dusty journals, beyond believing, the charlatans exposed with accomplices and ropes, wires wrapped around their toes, disembodied plaster hands whisked out from their robes to shake hands with the credulous believers eager to be deceived and thus to avoid the nameless blackness of unknowing, the wall of God's silent indifference to suffering. As if She would speak in English, when all of Her creation speaks more eloquently already of hope and rebirth, of arbitrary savagery and necessary survival, than any human rival could contrive in words. It is human echoes that the dial I turn upon my chest will hear, like a radio scanning the airwaves, playing the ancient stones of this abode like a vinyl record pricked with a pin. Oh the dim din of the ague of ages.

Robert says that he sends his love to little Bell and Jell, his nicknames for the children...

This time it is old Emily who nods her head vigorously, while Gladys endeavours to be a good girl, unable to sever the strict gaze of Horace, the old bespectacled owl, fixed upon her fevered brow in the dim light. The stone speaks and I tune into the voices of Robert and Horace, raised in an argument, the week before he set sail, then sense the brooding silence, the turbulence in both their heads afterwards. *He went to the waves, unreconciled with his father. You fought, Robert and you, Horace, harsh words, three days before he sailed, and failed to make up. He asks for your forgiveness and understanding. On the upstairs landing, the worst of it took place, you with your hand on the banister, he with the light from the attic window on his face.*

Horace has sat up rigid at the first mention of this, but now I see his head bowed in strange tension and shame. *On the subject of his inheritance... six thousand pounds he sought to borrow to pay for another boat... the words of begging sticking in his throat, a failure in your eyes in these difficult times. He begs again your forgiveness for these crimes.*

No! Enough of this impudence! Horace stands and bellows, his composure ashen white and jaundiced yellow. *This is intolerable! Who has been sharing their gossip with this impostor in our home?!* Emily, aghast at his chair thrown back, covers her mouth and babbles and weeps all in one unintelligible scribble upon the air, while Gladys rings her hands, festoons her hair in deranged bunches, and only the children hit a simpler tone: crying and wailing quietly, less at the supernatural air than at their grandparent's deranged behaviour.

I find myself mouthing a prayer to our saviour Jesus, the last that passed poor Robert's lips as the distant waves come close and lift me by the hips, pushing on the table and knocking away my wheelchair. *Our father who art in Heaven, keep safe my beloved Gladys, Annabel and Nigel...*

Mummy, mummy, Nithna is flying! Look! He is flying! – Little Nigel shrieks, more enchanted now than scared, while his sister's hair lifts up as of its own accord, charged with crackling electricity.

But I am not flying but drowning. More Stevie Smith than Robert Browning. More disappointed than uplifted by Nature's wonders frowning on my blunders. Thunder, lightning, lashing of rain and gales. My limbs flail. I cry out. I am lifted up until I float above the table, writhing in blue mist rippling, water filling my lungs in involuntary gulps, the loss of air crippling, my mind going dim as the pain in my chest passes beyond the bearable, the table thrown against the wall, and all my audience cowering away before the grotesque display of a man defying gravity. Levity, literally, importunately but fortunately also: brevity, the nearest window smashing, unable to withstand the severity of proximity to my thrashing extremities. Out, out, I am blown, with the few brief candles left, by one last ghostly wave from beyond the grave, to the comparative safety of a freezing December night, landing in soft snow and waking sharply looking outside-in upon the forlorn domestic glow of which I know I must now take my leave. Unbelievably cold, the ice upon my outstretched palms, but relievingly useful to a man without full use of his disobedient legs. I scramble and tumble then rumble out across the ice, my jacket bunched-up below like a makeshift toboggan, groggy, walk like a doggy, thrashing froglike, then devising a method out of desperate necessity to propel me face-down across the ice. Oh thank you kindly obliging moon so nearly full as to prove a useful tool, God-held torch to light my path. Behind me, dimly, I hear figures shifting in disarray, attempting pursuit but recoiling in dismay at the greater danger that their lesser footprints represent, stiletto point-loads of boots producing fissures and cracks, held back by all the focussed weight I lack. Hocus pocus, practical application of the levitation tack, I'm mastering the knack, just don't look back. To surge with adrenalin bubbling in my ears, to differentiate between the tears of loss or rage I seek to leave behind me, for an age, for years.

My arms thrash and I progress famously towards another island and some gladsome pile of junk, a veritable trunk of treasure for my pleasure to secrete myself within at my leisure, a tether of old boats and nets and tarpaulins in which to smother my memory of all human blether, severing the bindings of consciousness, falling, falling into sleep instead, caressed with thankyous of the dead for the brief bridge of net I weave to let them have their say. At last I reach the shore and grab up onto the planks of a swaying boat and lever myself aboard, and covering myself over: snore, snore until I am no more. A door closing over, losing all connection with what is to come and what has been before.

*

How much time goes by? In sleep, we live and die the forgotten lives of centuries. When I awake, from deep exhaustion and ache in my arms, my first task and trick is to prise the mask off my face, done quick, several months too late. The noise abates of who I was, my blood deflates before the gates of possibility. And finally, after suitable repose, I stand up, under cover of night once more, and walk, walk on firm and sweetly crunching shores, my knees tender at first, as if new to this art of bending. Bones shudder as if rending. The sinews tighten, the muscles obey their old logic, rediscovering habit. I sway, nearly stumbling, mumbling, grumbling, but at length am on my way with regained strength. My head, mouth open to drink the chill night air, rejoices at regaining its former altitude redolent of natural attitude and rectitude of limbs. A glimmer of light in the night ahead draws me on and I keep walking, talking to myself, until dawn.

*

I wake again. Island after island. This place is tiring. Ice breakers have been through now in the larger channels. Crunch, crunch, brittle and dirty shards bunched up like toffee icing. Steam rising from shouting mouths. Accosting boatmen, I barter some of the good flannels on my back for the money I lack to pay for the crossings, turning and tossing, grabbing old rags and tarpaulins instead for clothing, reverting to self-loathing. At last I leave behind the rash of various trivial skerries serviced by ferries for a landmass of respectable size and semblance of sophistication, civilisation. I step out of the boat and walk up into some streets of discreet charm, panache and élan. And passing my reflection in a shop window, recall who I am. No easy question or answer to a man on the run from himself pursuing his phantom semblance and terrible twin. Again therefore, let me begin:

Let me in! I rap on the glass of a window I pass. Shucking fight! What ridiculous quirk of shirking fate is this? Squirting piss, I'm irate. Inside, hung up on walls like appalling crucifixions, a spectacle apt to exhaust my extensive diction: are seven paintings I recognise as my own. My, my, such a long way from home. I'm suddenly all erect as a dog with a bone, and of a mind to be direct and as tenacious as this gallery is spacious. Specious and facetious. In time, the world-wearied owner of grey hair and half-moon spectacles makes his way to the door and hoists the blinds with his liver-spotted tentacles. *I am the artist!* –is the only ridiculous appeal I can muster through the glass, all fart and bluster. And to my surprise, not for the first time in these travails through tearful vales, I am treated to the unexpected good in human nature threatening to unravel my settled scepticism. Get knotted nihilism! The old guy unlocks his door though I must resemble the worst of the threatening poor, and offers me a place by a fire in his back room where he makes me coffee and sweeps the floor with a broom as if I am some prince come out of the darksome night carrying the light of the world through all the days of winter. Such kindness. *You believe,* I stammer, *–that I, Ithir, am as I claim, the author of these paintings? Such blind faith has me close to fainting!*

Only guesswork is blind, my friend, and faith is something else entirely different and inspiring. For here... he brings a painting to me taken from the walls, *–is evidence that I do not guess, nor do you lie, at all.*

And there sure enough, written rough but clear in queer handwriting not my own, is the name Ithir The Rhymer, dated last year. How strange, perhaps those arty types in Industria did not turn clypes as might be expected after I was last rejected and ejected, but valued my work on its own merits after the dust had settled, and stashed it away like ferrcts. Or more likely, as this current outing has me doubting, hooded it in cloth but brooded on it nightly, then sold it proudly as the work of a new artist of note, not the usual copyist of Dirze.

Yes... my host muses, eavesdropping my mind, anticipating my line of thoughts like ink blots, introducing himself as one Mustafa Hakim, *...your work shows the influence of Dirze alright, but you are your own man. The world is tiring of his work, among sophisticated circles at least, self-referential and self-indulgent as he grows, whilst yours is leaner, keener and meaner, one might propose: a whole new style for a future suture of the wound of the past, a dark century drawing to a close. Don't quote me now, these my private thoughts I hasten to disclose.*

I am speechless. A rare condition for me. And penniless and clueless (not so rare). *How come you trusted such a threadbare apparition as me to let me over the threshold of your locked door?*

Mustafa smiles, his eyes hooding in modesty in the firelight. *I was an immigrant once, helpless as you, off the boat from furthest Asia, and yet good people sheltered me as I see now that God has granted me the opportunity to do for you. Nearly fifty years ago. So warm your toes. My faith teaches that hospitality is a great honour and obligation, when one comes asking of it in such abject misery and desolation as you. I see myself and my salvation in your situation, for without giving freely how can we accept what is given freely unto us? Some huge hand above us writes up the tally of all our lives in his ledger, always moving and writing, and though his calculations spin far as stars beyond our mortal ken, this I know: that to receive happiness we must give happiness, and that this alchemy is the opportunity we are all put on earth to do.*

Dark though the winter morning outside lurks, I weigh Mustafa's recipe and calculate on balance that I buy it, indeed it probably works, I can't deny it, should I ever try it. The man is no dewy-eyed fool, but has plans afoot already to help me find my feet, discreetly calculating my capabilities and options, my potential function with the utmost unction. *Luncheon!* He exclaims, *I am to meet an artist this week, and with a lift of the phone I could make the date today and bring you with me anyway, to introduce, to start as his assistant, understudy and paint-mixer. He's the real thing, an honest impoverished artist and no trickster. You get my drift? Move swift and true, work hard as I know an immigrant like you will do, and you will have access to paints and easels. Weasel yourself in there and you could soon have new work of your own, lurking in the studio recesses, of which I must confess I'd like regular perusal and first refusal.*

Your kindness shames a knave such as I, who has so signally failed hitherto to try to apply himself to humanity's everyday endeavours, shirking responsibility to the best of my abilities, quick to sever ties despite the sighs of those I leave behind to despise me. Size me up if you must, but do not trust the scallywag that lurks inside this raggle taggle gypsy. Tipsy, all too often. Soften not your heart, lest this scoundrel break it apart. I am a bad lot, sir, to summarise, a sight for sore sighs, from end to start. But there is more, I must confess without duress, in the presence of your kindness. I harbour hatred in my heart for my brother, who I pursue with ill-intent to do him in. Jealousy I dare say, for all the good fortune that has favoured him rather than me since we were both grasshopper knee-high, if a shin. A twin with which I have often tussled, and our muscles well-matched we have well-nigh seen the other off to hell more often than I dare tell and more often recently. Indecently sore and near to death's door how I left him last. Aghast, bereft of him likely, one night soon.

Mustafa laughs aloud but sadly, seeing through me with old wisdom. *You lack confidence like a child, traumatised by the wild life you've led. But banish and put behind you all the baggage of the years. You crossed this threshold with no past that I need or wish to hear. These paintings which I see are yours betray a soul more sensitive and astute than the one your description parodies for my ears. Besides, these dread turmoils which you describe are classic fodder with which the tortured artist can exploit his fears for fruitful seasons. These are reasons to paint, and not to be faint-hearted. Once you and your art are united, you'll not be parted. Choose this chance and complete what you have started. In self-esteem through toil you can redeem your soul and thence spare your poor brother all your erstwhile ire. His only sin it seems is to have had god smile upon him, therefore the squabble you pick is with yourself. For god has smiled on you also, but you were too envious to see it. To be blessed in this world you must first know what a blessing is and how to accept it.*

You are more like a priest or a mystic than a gallery owner. How comes such an oddity about? I am a lout, but amongst the crowd you are more a shepherd than a ticket tout.

Who knows what ways the winds of fate blow each of us about? Take this new hat and coat on loan. I will see you out, walk about our island until noon then meet me at the café by the harbour where I'll introduce you to the artist I've described. After we a few glasses have imbibed I'm sure he'll take you under his wing. It's just the thing, such good luck this tide that to our island Ithir brings, to join the tribe of artists, the noblest minstrels to nature's praises sing.

Church bells ring as I step out onto the cobbles and hobble through the piled up snow. Strangely revived, heart beating, my blood heating me from inside, I regain my stride and perambulate this pretty town as would the usual tourist. Fine Hanseatic brick and pediments, all pointed lintels and dentils and finicky mimicking of maritime details: iron gibbets from gables and stables, lofts for merchant storage and portage. Delicate fretwork painted iron railings and balconies and external staircases cascading like the unfolding parasols of delectable ladies, falling like dropped hankies to the street below, deigning to dare you to pick up the rhythm, quick, quick slow. All picked out nicely in white ice highlights by the celestial artist in meteorological modus operandi, glissandi: this still-lightly falling mist of snow, steady as she goes, crystals as shifting sifting petticoats crackling, each microscopic particle spinning like a ballerina in full flow. I am spun as in a grand dance down an avenue of partners before I am given away and let go. The music of Mozart or Strauss orchestrates and delineates the shop displays and alleyways, the exuberant renaissance order, soberly on show.

Quaysides and boats and capstans and thick-ply ropes are never far away, and well-used; never far from frayed. The leaded glass windows in the Corn Exchange make light glimmer like candles, glimpsed shimmerings of winter silver. Fortunes rising and falling with the tide of history. Blackened gothic pinnacles and buttresses above, like those on the cathedral, dark accretions of carved craftsmanship, smoked, sailing, dangling, as the golden balls of the pawnshops, gold ships of the merchants' domes and spires, the skyline vies for attention from the divine like a line of hawkers and talkers all pining and miming for our coins and our time. It is no crime, I assure myself, merely to wander and enjoy the clamour of haggle and bargain in passing, as a boat myself a-sail, meandering through myriad islands on which one has no interest in alighting, preferring the flighting, a snake of motion pursuing its own tail.

And thus happily, distractedly, do I pass my morning in preparation for the promised appointment, my newly-blistered feet (laid up for weeks) in urgent need of ointment. To the harbour then I wander lastly as the snow stops and the weak sun at its paltry zenith tears the gossamer grey cloud like winter woollens, and the thought of melting replaces pelting. *This is Kenneth Astley Kettering...* Mustafa introduces, loosing hither and thither the flaming arrows of his sparkling gaze, to spear at us both. *And this is Ithir The Rhymer or so he calls himself these days. I anticipate you two artistic bohemians will have much to say to each other, like unto brothers of the painting, roving trade.*

Then begins the tirade of Kettering's outpourings, appetite-whetting whitterings, as Mustafa seats us in a shiveringly off-season café perched at the water's edge, frozen condensation dripping from the window ledge:

Pleased to meet you, old man, Mustafa tells me you'd make a perfect apprentice, being a painter tentatively taking his early steps late in life, unburdened by a wife but rich in inspiration. Emancipation in the techniques of mixing paints and stretching canvases and even framing are the skills I'm naming in this jolly offer. Not that the wages shall be apt to line your coffers, being next to nothing but bed and board, still not to be ignored, sniffed, spat or scoffed at. All in all well worth the time of day to doff your hat at, wouldn't you say that?

And pray, what would you say, dear reader, were you ever desperate and destitute as I? Wouldn't you rather take a job without pay than languish in such freezing poverty as like to die? Say nay now and meet my eye. Not so? Thought so. We are not so different, you and I. Over hot broth, quaffed slow as a sloth, I doth quoth my troth to this harebrained serfdom for the promise of respectability, a tradesman, to the best of my meagre ability. But Mustafa smirks I surmise, knowing that Kettering will have a cuckoo crowing every sunrise, an artist greater than himself in the making, watching, learning, waiting from the wings, his stifled urge to sing not long abating.

Hands are shaken on it, then Kettering dons his jaunty bonnet, being very much the archetypal arty type, more apt to write a Shakespearian sonnet than waste time cogitating on it. And we follow him through the cobbled streets, huddled now against an icy north wind, to reach his creaking antiquated attic, up many stone steps worn by the boots of centuries. *Do you know...* he opines over his breezy shoulder from above us ascending, that these lodgings were once the abode of Pintorello? Holy smoke and liberate the ghetto! Robed angels from heaven bending down to pluck their harps of gold, I am enchanted as of old to hear this brag, backed-up by a plaque upon the brickwork, warmed by such knowledge against the fiercesome cold, as if a fire were lit inside me. Rattle of ancient keys in the iron lock, creaking nudging of ship hulls moored in the dock, we are inside soon and gathered round the hearth and mantelpiece eyed by a solitary clock to navigate the ages. And we three sages are arrived at the nascent rout of the complacent, the birth of an artist fit to recover the renaissance. I mean myself of course. Not lacking, despite the act, self-regard or the necessary patience.

We find ourselves inside a tall attic roof criss-crossed by beams, much bigger than it seems, a veritable Noah's ark in which to flee the winter's dark, creaking in the wind as an ancient galleon beached upon these shores, an echo-chamber for Kettering's snores, as I am treated to later on that night, as into the upper timbers I take flight and hang my hammock. But before that: we part with Mustafa on the steps outside, his eyes confiding that he sees me as the prize with which to buy his way to heaven. One so uncomplicatedly deserving of his alms in my palms without qualms being surprisingly hard to find, short of the lame and blind. I am honoured by his charity, or more precisely: his faith in me.

As through a tree, each night and morn now I descend and ascend through the spars and rafters of the trusses holding up this medieval roof. Forsooth, when my hours of mixing paints are done and I am spied by none, Kettering being gone out along the quays to take the sea breeze, I feed my wires into the old stone walls and rotate my dial as if to search for Radio Luxembourg. Radio Thanatos more like, a wavelength thronged with voices, and there I find old Pintorello himself sooner or later, son of a dyer, rebuked by academia, who chose instead the harder self-taught route. God loves a tryer. A town-crier, charged with desire, whose lit fire could not be extinguished by all the grey sea of envy that rippled around him daily like ruffled feathers. In every weather, he paced these streets, living and dressed but simply as a peasant, to draw and paint scenes dramatic and pleasant. Then portraits, of patrons by steps more influential by the year, boosting the credentials of this queer misfit resolutely non-compliant and self-reliant. A giant to history, and as such men often are: but an apparent dwarf in life to the apparent dwarves that surrounded him. A slim glimmer lights the way to genius. It is the task of those who would follow such a path to find the strength to wander unaccompanied through the long and thankless dark, the challenge stark. Hark, hark, the distant hunting horn of Apollo, the lyre of Orpheus. Pay no heed to idiocy, but follow your Eurydice.

Mustafa visits every second day then once a week. His demeanour kind, his manner meek. Encouraging me in my studies under Kettering to consolidate my mysterious abilities, seemingly unlearned or borrowed from some previous life. With a palette knife I learn to restrain my violent passions and harness them to more considered lashings of paint, and observe the industry and discipline with which Kettering approaches each work, taking time to catch each fragment of inspiration where it lurks and not rush the whole enterprise into compromise. Mustafa my friend, accompanies me on walks at each day's end, and although his faith will not permit him a drop of alcohol we learn not to let this come between us at all, but go instead to visit all the island's grand palaces and churches to stand and wonder, then at last to his mosque where he bids me kneel and pray with him each day. We dare to say that the God we each spin in awe of, lectures in architecture, our eyes lifted to each carved and singing detail, exalting the dead overhead, is the same deity inspiring piety and easing anxiety. It is in the everyday that we will find the way to Him, Mustafa preaches, in a thousand small steps towards the sacred reaches.

Then just when I begin to dare to believe my inner demons bested, ever-wary fate sets its snares to have me tested. Word reaches the artistic loft of Kettering and Ithir of a controversial exhibition opening soon to whose private view but a few local bohemians are invited. The press are to be slighted, it seems, for their ignominious role in hindering this artist's plans to get himself knighted. His blighted career seeks to be re-ignited, his enemies indicted. You are right, dear reader, it is Dirze himself on which our narrative has once again alighted.

Kindly Kettering lends me a shirt, one unusually devoid of dirt or paint, and helps me trim my beard fit to make the ladies faint. Then before Mustafa can warn us off, dressed as a dandy and a toff we set out from our loft to walk the several blocks and canals to where the party's planned. Kettering can't understand my seeming reticence in praising his eminence Dirze, dismissing all the media slander as irrelevant to his genius, and apt to get on his gander. But I remind him that it is the man himself who first wedded his fortunes to the media circus, drowning content in pout and portent. Sleet is falling as we briskly go, to and fro between the ebb and flow of the rivers of people and water stirred at eventide, the Oceania citizens intent on retiring to where they each habitually reside. As Kettering talks, I watch their million eyes and long to confront them with my prize: my many paintings planned and underway to show them to themselves, unmasked and nakedly displayed.

We arrive at last at a suitably vast disused warehouse at the cobbled quayside, its dirty windows dirtied some more of late with diluted whitewash to defy the avid critic's gaze. Our passes verified, we pass through a haze of chattering bodies, the old vernissage assemblage rife again, towards a small but welcome blaze held in an iron grate at the centre of the space, throwing an orange glow on each eager face which gravitates towards the warmth and nibbles on a plate. And yes, unfortunately, free glasses of the demon drink are also there displayed, in varieties and quantities profligate. The hubbub of conversation grows, as Kettering constantly darts around intercepting those he knows, and some kind fellows introduce themselves, fellow artists and a few gallery owners, my unaccustomed hand to shake, two types differentiable by their attire and demeanour, the first like Technicolor waifs, the second inflatable dirigibles tethered at the waist.

Music is provided, quietly in contrast to this cacophonic set, by four ladies of a string quartet performing Bach in mathematical precision with a certain frisson beside the disused gibbet of a packing hoist, the great black hook hovering over them like the deathly symbol in a parable of choice. Promising ascension to an exalted dimension. Attention! Into this demented noise a voice makes an unexpected incision. And then suddenly there is Dirze, received not yet with derision but still with an air of awe apt to make the acolyte paw, attended by a flock of black-dressed priestesses in glamorous dresses and coiffured tresses, fanning out like pickpockets to seep through the crowd and then; at his signal reach up and remove each shroud from off his surrounding canvases. Glasses are put down so that the masses can gasp and then applaud, gawping at the sudden visual onslaught encircling them like wagons. I reach for further flagons of ale, irked to think that Dirze has not yet failed, his much trailered descent into obscurity with all that it entails not yet arrived. My stomach jives, my entrails fester at the performance of this jester. His paintings, needless to say, all look like nothing new, the same re-hashes of his stale and steadily heady brew of garish hue and caricatured chiaroscuro. But what do I know?

But now for once my sick and addled mind fixates on something new. From amongst Dirze's slick entourage I begin to notice a face I cannot place, and yet whose beauty holds a curious weight, her lovely eyes and cheekbones resonate, as if I've nearly met her once before, but what occasion I cannot calculate. I fixate, cogitate, try to look away, but catching my gaze, to my astonishment she reciprocates. And over several minutes by way of circuitous social rounds and routes with intervening parties, we contrive to glide together without a sound and there by the burning grate to achieve a slight collision followed by apology, unction and introduction. Collusion, this illusion of two strangers met by chance, culmination of a balletic dance by flickering firelight. Pathetic affettuoso melody is struck up virtuoso at this moment by the feminine quartet as further fate. We talk, stuck fast as needles on a record to rotate about each other, sister and brother, bathed each in the light flowing from the other.

I tell her of my artistic aspirations and inspiration, and bit by bit she lowers her voice and whispers close to tears of the last dismal year she's spent in the company of the dreaded Dirze, touching my wrist repeatedly to remind me that all this is in strictest confidence and imprudence, but that his impudence can no longer pass without remark and incident. *He drinks heavily you know, more and more, before and after every show, consumed with terror as to how things will go. And his mounting debts mount higher than anyone can know. And as to my wages, well, I am ashamed to say I should have left his employment long ago, but hang around as do the other girls, in the hope that we'll be paid late at last and taken up again in the swirl and froth and frills of an exciting life of exotic travel and popping pills. But what's the use? Perhaps I envy you your basic existence of artistic persistence, free from the pestilence of wealth that threatens human health. I am an artist too you know, a student of drawing and painting once, but like a dunce I've let that man parade me for my looks alone and turn my sorry heart to stone.*

Cold though the night is, to hear ourselves better over the buzzing fizz of talk around us, we walk out onto the quayside and sit on a capstan each, to preach each to each our plans to transform our lives and shed our former skins. *You are so beautiful...* I venture, *in this mysterious maritime illumination, if you would forgive my voicing such an indiscreet rumination.*

Her eyebrows lift. *Oh that old chestnut. How tedious to be judged constantly by one's looks. Do you and other men suffer the incessant indignity of the knives of stares? Yet some women must it seems, and is that fair? To be hunted and observed everywhere, insidiously and unawares? I am like a mobile statue with a living soul entombed inside, and all the fools I meet project their childish fantasies and dreams onto this blank canvas which is not me at all, but just the accidental shell that I am wrapped up within. Our appearance is but a random roll of dice, and yet the shallow Pierrots of this world pursue this phantom half their lives, descending into vice on its account. If this is life as God intended, then politely, prithee, count me out.*

Such words of truth to hear at last from such a mouth is a relief enough to make me shout with joy. Her sad eyes gaze worldly wise, world weary and austere, through me to the core as none before and I at last have nowhere left to hide. *I must confide you speak as one who has sneaked into the attic of my head and read the diary of my mind...* I reply in shock, *I have been blind to the possibility that a soul as lost as I could be hidden so close at hand, and we could wander unknown to each other forever through this darkened land. But aren't some men likewise cursed by the adoration of girls frivolous and shallow, fixating on their matinee idol surface, entirely unaware of the depths, pleasant or unpleasant, which wash in waves below, resounding between unknown shores? Do not despair, for surely there is hope and grandiosity in*

Nature's plan that has spanned so many millennia to bring us to this here and now as never before?

Perhaps, but higher genius though reality may yet be, let us not suppose that it is of necessity symmetrical... She answers, tilting her head as to weigh it all with scales calibrated and metrical, *We have but one heart each for instance, and it does not sit at our centre, nor do the appendix and spleen. All is skewed, perverse, adrift and obscene in the obscure constellation of human life, a project underway on the scaffold of the universe, too vast for any perspective to reveal. Women by and large, listen to the voice behind the mask, while men see no further than its surface and do not think to ask. What is the task then? —the grand enterprise of which we all fall short? The ultimate gesture and last resort?*

My retort is of a sort not verbal or ineffectually intellectual but instinctual for a pleasant change: I find that I have done something deranged and taken her in my arms and kissed her. The dockside mist like a clouding of the brain swirls in slow drifts around us as I vanish blissfully into this sustained osculation. Wheeling of stars across the heavens and aggregation of centuries like sediment. From my mortal impediment I am freed and chained all at once by the spark of concern that once lit burns in the brain and floods the veins of two organisms reaching out towards each other, two trees straining to intertwine their branches. Both enflamed and drained in the aftermath, I discover something astonishing as we withdraw and pull away: a loud cracking noise, a shudder and a shiver, as if all the mechanistic cogs of physics are giving way in dismay. With not a little pain and confusion we see that both our faces, interlocked and bonded, have now peeled away. My damaged metal mask, impacted into hers, and now both falling to the cobbles in disarray. Crash, crumple, gasp and tumble. Our reaching hands encounter and entangle each other's, bending over. And looking up, what do we see now of each other's true appearance? Eyes widening, nearing revelation, our disparate throats break into ululation.

But the warehouse doors are thrown open, light spilling out in sickly yellow degradation, our recent scene sullied by observation. Dirze's retinue of hired muscle emerge and tussle with my Aphrodite before I've even caught her name. And pushing me back, administer to me the same brutal treatment. Defeat, even in the moment of triumph. I cry out after her, but get a fist in my face to focus my thoughts and my dental health plan. Second-best as ever to my dread brother. *Where are you headed with her, you fuckers?* –I shout, spitting out a canine and a molar. Hands over her mouth, she is dragged away kicking, but her eyes meet mine one last time. And that is enough to determine my mission, for all eternity.

Bleeding and stumbling, mumbling profanity and inanity, I pursue as best I can along the many quays and piers that Dirze's demons make their retreat along. One even produces a gun, a few blocks along once we've left the throng, and shatters the brickwork of each doorway that I duck inside and hide in. Until gaining ground they reach a harbour with the tide in and all flee on board a boat and hoist their anchor. The wankers. No doubt Dirze himself is in the cabin at the centre of their infernal machinations, poring over a nautical chart and devising some new stratagem of the heart and soul to confound my longing. But he bolts the stable door too late, and fate it seems has turned the tide. For wounded and breathless as I am, and collapsed at the water's edge, now I have glimpsed my salvation in another soul tormented as myself. Now I am deathless and where once I was outcast, I understand belonging. I am of this world again at last, and destined to master it. Do not ask one who has once tasted it to abandon it: the elixir of life I mean, unleashed between two beings, which opens a door to immortality, the ability to transcend and escape our sordid physicality. Undaunted, I climb down a harbour ladder and steal myself a boat and paddle, and although I may be slow and addled by fog, with hard slog I will achieve my goal I know. I will never be alone again, and this thought gives me the strength of ten men and the patience of a hundred. I set sail, and will not fail to regain the treasure my brother has plundered. I shall grace these shores no more. When night next lifts its veil, I will be in Sylvia.

~

PART FOUR

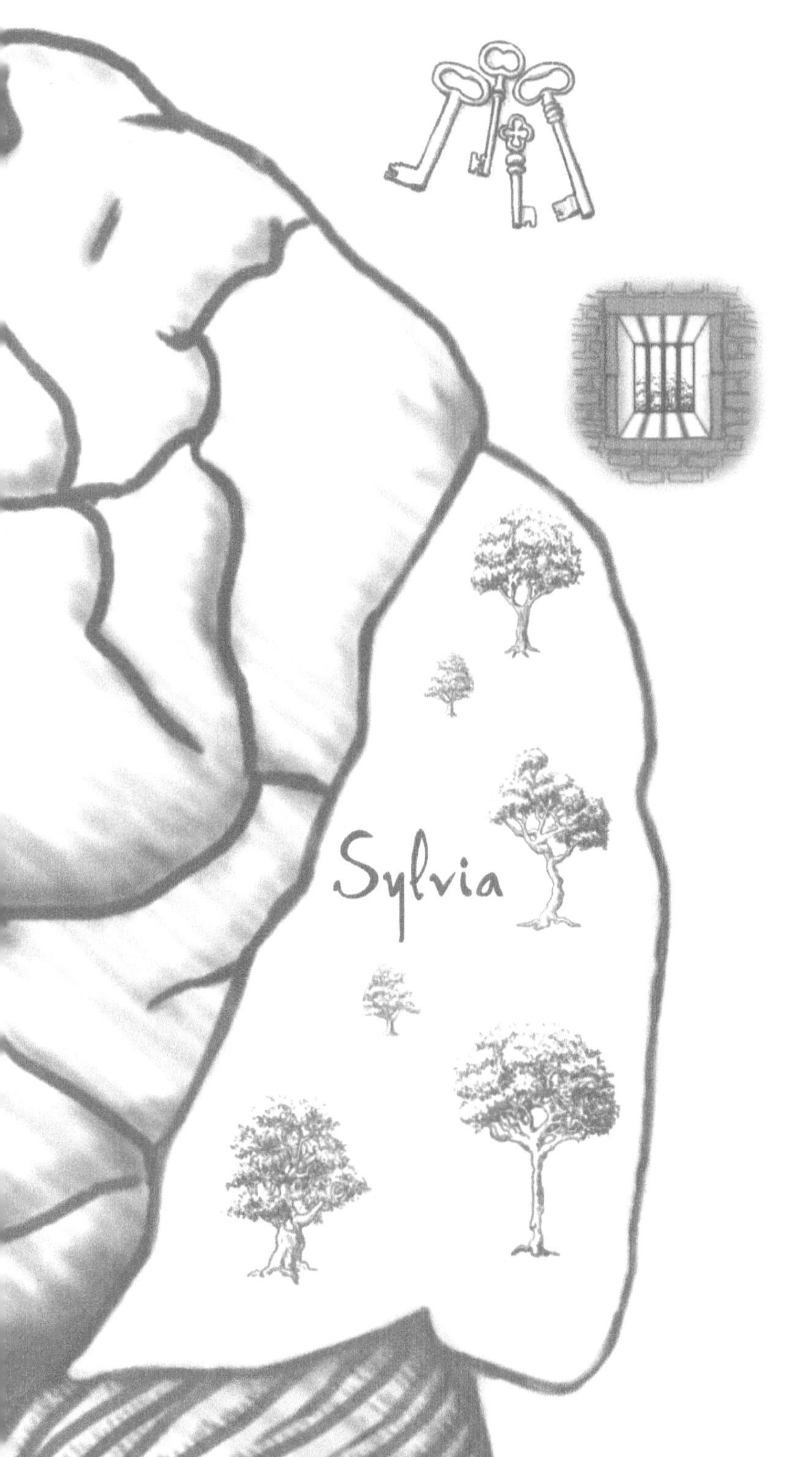
Sylvia

Swishing of tree leaves. A forest breathing like an enormous lung. I wake up and am overjoyed to find a shingle shore crunching under my beached rowboat, and immediately stand up and fall over. Sea legs extraordinaire, I am debonair for all of the two seconds that my limbs can bear, then violently sick, pebble-dashing the pebble-dash. I have reached land at last, after many days adrift between the maddeningly myriad islands of that watery suburb behind me to find myself here, here. But it is queer to see trees and cliffs and mountains again, the glorious glens and valorous valleys. Have they missed me as I them? Again, I try to stand, and faring better, take my first steps on dry land. Then turning to take my leave of the ocean's mirror, I recall with a shiver that I have lost my face and have no idea yet as to with what it has been replaced. I retrace my paces then kneeling find a pool of still water in a quiet space and wait, wait… for the breath of the breeze to cease and reveal to me who I am. There kneels a man, a lot like me, unshaven and dishevelled, with a backdrop of trees. He seems vaguely familiar, but a mirror is an inversion, a perversion, a carnival trick. Only the girl with whose face I collided has seen where my soul resided. Oh that we might have had long enough so that in me she confided.

Pine trees everywhere, evergreen and deciduous, evoking residual religiosity, tall as the pillars of a cathedral nave or choir, but I stand at the crossing now I sense, enchanted with Nature's incense, the smell of sap from porous bark. Hark, is that a singing bird I hear? Spring, if not already here, is near. No more to fear, I will banish winter darkness from my soul's long year. For I have found my Aphrodite and seen the hope to banish all my tears. And if I found her once, I know I may again. But what of men? They occur everywhere, spontaneous as trees, half so useful and less inclined to please. An infestation of every nation, they try my patience. And as I pick my way over roots and rocks, I see a roadway not far off enough, and realise with tired eyes and sighs that I must interact with humankind again. Onward, then. Headfirst into the lion's den, the dread domain of men.

Hard-packed stones then tarmacadam, over many miles, if truth be told, do much to reconcile my heels and toes to the comforts of the road, as opposed to the rolling mulch of roots and leaf mould. And picking up a pace, oh joy, I am no longer cold, but nurtured sweetly by spring springing in its buds and shoots all around me, the tweeting of birds alighting in branches, delighting and astounding. They fill my soul with music of sweet anticipation, and adrift on Nature's tides I am as a refugee arriving at the borders of Her nation, my passport the memory of the face and voice of Aphrodite. I will be part of life, its orbiting satellite no longer. The sun shall feed my hunger.

An unfortunate metaphor perhaps, for all too soon I feel an ache in my knee-caps fit to lead me to collapse, and reaching the outskirts of a town, lest I fall down, find my way to the first available tavern and sit myself down. I say a town and yet the effect is more as if the occasional cottage in the surrounding woods have multiplied and aggregated in number by slow degree until there might be said to be more brick than timber, and tiles than leaves. Tall trees abound in Sylvia and its populaces show their faces as might squirrels and foxes or birds in boxes, peeping that is, upon one's business, before returning to their profits and losses. *Can I help you sir?* −A portly barman intones from some height upon my exhausted limbs, and I eye him apprehensively before suggesting my age-old jest, a test to see if he'll buy my bargain. *Have you a musical instrument,* I hazard, *a violin say, or a flute, a cor anglais, oboe or violoncello? A pianoforte, harpsichord, or clavichord?*

The fellow's brows furrow as rainclouds gathering to ransack a mountain top. He opens his mouth in wrinkling perplexity, but I continue for him: *Or a virginal, muselar or spinet perhaps? A terpodion, uranion or melodion? A penny whistle?* Now his eyebrows lift and he tries so speak again but is thwarted by my further interjection: *Or a celesta, an octobass, or lira da braccio? A kazoo would do, or even a jew's-harp or harmonica? I've even been known to fetch a tune on a twelve-inch ruler or wineglass with a wetted finger. Fair enough, I can see I'm getting nowhere so I shall not linger...*

Wait! –Cries out an eaves-dropper before I come a proper cropper, standing up with the barman's hands grappling for my collar. *Can you play an accordion?*

A squeeze box, by crikey, why do I always overlook the most likely? *Throw one my way and I shall entertain you mightily and cordially, accordingly.* Phew… food and drink I think and a pile of straw to recline on nightly. I hoist the heavy instrument of enlightenment and set the grace notes spinning to cancel out my imminent indictment for vagrancy. Like ripples, I soon marvel at the waves of sound lapping at the surrounding ears and passing on out into vacancy. The human soul is constantly astir it seems, enflamed as an itching skin, and fond of being soothed by an external agency. Eternal exigency, this soporific balm to calm the savage breast or suck its nipple like a tipple famed for its astringency, smelling salts, the brandy glass, the draught liqueur for all contingencies. Awaken! And in its wake, we are each uplifted, reminded of the divine elixir for which we are all vessels. Wrestle no more, but let it in, let it pour.

Then in the door, after four hours or more, forty-six tunes, three pints and two legs of boar, there walks a face I can't quite place, some unextinguished acquaintance relinquished from before. Distinguished? By Jove, yes! It's the good Doctor Horace Stockbridge, bedecked with dishevelled spectacles upon his nose, and looking a little morose, indeed in need of refreshment and repose. *The state of your clothes!* I intone, nearly standing on his toes, *What roughshod tangle you've been dangled in, do please now hasten to disclose…*

Do I know you? –He responds, wide-eyed. And of course I've half forgot the morbid procedure by which I periodically change my facial features. What a strange creature I am. Inimical inimitable physiognomical anomaly.

You used to get on with me. And indeed took me into your home. My name then was Nithna or some such blether. But I am averse to being tethered to arbitrary nomenclature or sedentary leisure. Peripatetic being my pathetic epithet of preference. Do forgive me if I've invaded your privacy and shot to fuck your frame of reference. It is good to see you again, Doctor. I beg forgiveness for my hasty exit stage left last and thank you heartily for all your kindness of the past.

Nithna?

Nadir, they seem to call me here now. Queer, I know, all this ebb and flow of labelling. I'll be tabling an amendment to the central committee, if I ever find one, on this and many other topics, before I go into that goodnight and all that shite. What brings you here tonight into this prefecture, and in such a state of sartorial dishevelment?

It is you! I'd know your incessantly obsessive rhyming any time and anywhere, your alliteration in any nation, your onomatopoeia in any...

Come, come, Doctor, you can leave the verbal athletics to me, we wouldn't want our audience to think us a pair of epistemological epileptics, would we?

Quite so... And Stockbridge looks around over the bridge of his nose and spectacles held on with loose elastic, observing that he has become the spectacle at last now the music's lapsed. The bar customers are all agape to hear at last a clue of my identity and his. Well, I'd sooner piss in their glasses. *Follow me and we shall quaff our ale outside where we can escape the venal ears of these loutish lads and admire instead the asses of passing lassies.*

Toss it back, the cold beer splashes. Stockbridge I surmise is in some mess stickier than a barrel of molasses. Hands shaking he asks: *Lassie's asses? You never spoke like that before, Nithna. Have your dormant drives been awakened or am I mistaken? Some incident of intimacy, oceanic or obscene, drawn your attention to the primal scene?*

Ahh doctor, your perspicacity is greatly penetrating to the point of gratingly enervating. Next you'll be asking how often I'm masturbating. Truth be told I did encounter a certain girl who set my poor love-parched soul a whirl on another island of your archipelago, but no sooner were we matched than she was snatched by a batch of my dread brother's brutes to return her to his nefarious seraglio. My fate was sealed by that intaglio. And so I found myself here, pursuing the boat that stole my Aphrodite. I pine for her nightly, unsure now how to find her, except perhaps to track my sibling, dribbling avaricious demon that he is, dripping semen from his three foot penis. But enough of my deranged estrangement and failed amorous arrangements, what of you, good doctor? –

You seem more out of sorts than me, to whom such resorts to desperation are merely standard medication.

Good gracious, Nithna, your life is never simple. Your psychic state sounds positively stifling, besidé which my own predicament is trifling. I was merely mugged by thugs who I caught rifling through my case. They stole all my money, I'm told it's commonplace in this disreputable district. I've informed the authorities and given a description to the police who helpfully tell me it was all my fault for not using a padlock and leaving it unattended for enough milliseconds for them to have the thing upended. I was insured, so bar a few minor injuries I am inured to the whole sorry escapade, and grateful they did not stick a stiletto in my aorta to sabotage my badinage. But anyway, the uncanny thing in all of this is the reason I came here on this ill-fated journey at all. It was because I came across a notice in a newspaper announcing a forthcoming exhibition here in Sylvia by a mysterious new artist masquerading under the name of Ithir The Rhymer. Curious moniker I thought, then I saw his cryptic biography and portrait, but by some wild trick of photography this artist looked like our Nithna, miraculous man from nowhere washed up on the shores of Oceania. So I packed my bags and set out to find you anticipating many enquiries and dead-ends then by some weird godsend, after a perfunctory mugging, the first tavern I stumble into has you, or you claiming to be you, your name and face all changed as by a wipe of the lens, quite deranged really this little set-to straight out of the blue. Just what am I to do? –Or to make of this, or this indeed? He brandishes a crumpled poster folded and rolled, whipped from his pocket and torn from a wall with which he's recently collided.

Jumping J-J-Jehoshaphat… I stammer, discomfited and disjointed to the point of fainting, casting my jaded peepers over an image of three of my own paintings, now I too am agape at the manic machinations of fate. I scan the small print for explanation of this situation and there in a corner spy two names that flick everything into focus, clearing the smoke of hocus pocus: *"Kenneth Astley Kettering and Mustafa Hakim request your company at an exhibition of their esteemed missing colleague, protégé and auteur manqué, Ithir The Rhymer, whose paintings have been hailed of late as 'heralding a new movement's vanguard" (– Scunthorpe Times Literary Standard)."*

You see? Stockbridge exults, steadying me now as much as I him, leaning together like a monument to muddleheadedness bifurcated at the shins. Slim, the sinew of reality to which we cling, which brings us on its whim in due course from one moment to the next and thence to enlightenment. *This is the very exhibition which I'm seeking out, no doubt, and you the maestro the world is hungry now to learn much more about...*

The world and Scunthorpe, so I see. The hyperbole of marketing never ceases to astound me. Ground me, before my head sails off across the sky like a nylon Hindenburg in search of a pylon. This is all very well and good, but I would rather find the aforementioned dame, find love than fame, set my brother straight in all his debauched and raucous games than stick around and wallow like a pig in mud in the newfound notoriety of my name.

Stockbridge puts a steadying claw upon my sleeve. *Back up, old man, the two are scarcely opposites but apposite in fact in extremis to the task at hand. Have you not seen the news? Your brother, if such he be, is held captive in this land, in a jail not far from here I hear, indicted for tax evasion, drug trafficking, conspiracy to battery, murder and myriad other peccadilloes. We can go and interview the scoundrel there...*

Interview? How so?

Ahah! But now you see the real reason why I risked the roughing up by those ruffians' hands in striving to retrieve a reprieve for my grievously onerous and laborious paperwork... Stockbridge produces an official and legalistic looking pink file from his tattered attaché case. *My contact in Switzerland, whom you may recall I alluded to in psychoanalytic sessions, while domicile at my erstwhile island abode... Erno Schwitzer, esteemed and well-connected as an enormous octopus with testicles everywhere...*

Tentacles.

Spectacles.

Wallet.

And watch, all deleteriously painful to squash. I have been mysteriously granted legal permission on Schwitzer's behalf to view the police files lodged here in this very prefecture, on the case of one Thomas Leermouth, supposedly deceased, disgraced, and defaced by a bullet to the hypothalamus, on which note we once again find common interest and intent, do we not? To go find your brother and the location of certain members of his entourage, whilst researching the identity of a man who may or may not be you?

Synchronicity indeed. Sly synecdoche, my brother as a sinful syndicate of interest to the police. On mnemosyne on the other hand, I am less keen, I mean more than a little loath to be proven a live dead man and slammed in the can, when here I am deadly alive and free to roam wheresoever I please and can. You get my meaning, man?

Yes, yes... Stockbridge muses, *I think I can. But be at peace, by and by. Twenty years dead exceeds Lord Lucan's alibi, though somewhat shy of Adolf Hitler's. Schwitzer merely has the scientific bloodhound's nose, not a Simon Wiesenthal's bold thirst for justice, and besides his patient-confidentiality and Hippocratic oath are quite the match for a Swiss banker's double gold standards. You shan't be putting your head in a noose so much as a highly useful lanyard.*

Thank you Doctor, for that briefly inexplicable tour of twentieth century European history. A mystery, your circumloquaciousness could come to rival my own spacious speciousness. Have you been in training? And do you not find the effort draining?

Like straining over a chamber pot without warning on a cold morning. Potty training. But come let us shake our shaking hands on this then. I surmise I have you half won over, or indeed have run you over, and that after three more ales we'll sleep like pigs in clover.

Back into the hostelry we go then, I to play the keys and draw the bow, pluck strings, make music and make merry as a ferryman to cross the river of night for my passengers' delight, as well I might. And one acquaintance re-made and a deal struck, we feel no more need to make sense and indeed make less and less as the evening progresses towards its blessed oblivion. Next day I wake with my head next to the feet of a not unappealing dolly who has robbed me of my lolly, with a hazy memory of riding pillion in a supermarket trolley. Sitting up for a painful second, I spy sprawled across the carpet at the bottom of the bed fully dressed: Doctor Horace Stockbridge out for the count and as good as dead. And judging by the thunder in my head, my tongue and feet like lead, I shan't be getting up to check his life signs soon and besides right now with sweating brow, would envy him and anyone else eternal rest.

*

Too soon then our pretty host disturbs our fragile repose, throws us our clothes while fixing her make-up in a cracked mirror. Making a guess I call her Carol, only to be told it is Karen, gruffly. Close enoughly. Building on this success, I move on to guess her profession as we make our procession down the stairs, opening with a careless stumble a broom cupboard answered by a mumble of two people engaged in fornication in flagrante, enraged, engorged and apt to up the ante. We close the door upon their antics, and take our fresh air with the romantics and innocents of this world, stepping out beneath the fresh blue sky with clouds unfurled.

Pausing, dusting down his crumpled suit, Stockbridge hurries in my pursuit. I turn and hoot: *Oh that your beloved Emily could see you besmirched thus head to foot at the portal of a house of ill repute.*

Good god, the good doctor splutters, *what profane act must you have fallen asleep engaged in with her foot, and what did she mean about having played your flute?*

Ah, the monotony of anatomy. These points are moot, I venture, and incidental to our main adventure. Let us ease our addled brains of strains and stresses, over a cup of something black and hot, (you still have some money, have you not?) —while we peruse those addresses of constabulary establishments likely to harbour news of my brother and his misused muse, and if it amuses you: that other business too, of who you think I am but err, for I am not, and even if I were, remember not a jot.

And so the great towering trees of Sylvia rise up about us in the spring breeze, as we pace her imposing avenues. So much trunk and foliage, it is as if the place were but a forest with a certain residue of bricks and mortar, pricks and slaughter, sex and death and bad breath, caught up in her retinue. Beech and maple, oak, birch and pine all intertwine with architecture which eschews the straight line in favour of a more curvaceous flavour, organic of a manic savour, all swirls and twirls and caryatids, nymphs and girls, volutes, parabolas, scrolls, ellipses, ovals and twists soft to the eye but hard to resist, even by trolls and proles and not scoffed at by toffs not entirely cold. All carved most cunningly in timber, stone and glass. More joy to the eye than pain in the ass. Art Nouveau for the nouveau riche, more quiche than filet mignon, more rococo gone loco than lean modernist beef.

What a relief when the caffeine washes down, to sit by a window and let the afternoon skies drown us in their painterly clouds which wet themselves and us occasionally and discreetly, moistening the leaves and pavements with a glowing highlight of gold. Nostalgia like neuralgia, it is as if I did indeed know this place of old, such is the bold progress my eyes and footsteps make through its woods and moods. It is all for the good perhaps, this eerie return I shall not spurn in favour of further self-ignorance and denial. Some great trial approaches its closing reaches, and I shan't recoil from its teaching and preaching, beseeching me to look into a darkened glass whose many glimpses I have not hearkened to as along its gallery I've passed. So in all lives, we do not pause or look enough as hastily we go, as if the destination ruled out all hesitation. And yet Thanatos guards the end of our every street and every row, a harvest moon or a child's balloon cut loose, and all wise and ancient it knows: there is no hurry that negates our obligation to look right and left and carefully, wherever we go. 'What have you learned?' will be the one question we find our endeavours have earned at Saint Peter's gate, and inattention seal our fate.

But what is this incessant imprint that crowds my eyes each time I blink? –The memory of the face and smiles and laughter of a girl. My rationale can transcend the strictures of this picture burned into my heart, and yet each time I drop my guard her image returns and burns and burns. Are we no more than arrows and darts loosed as sport from some mischievous bow from One on high who plays with us as toys, our terrors and joys mere spectacle for his cruel sport? Does each broken heart, as a gunshot register a loud report in that ethereal chamber overhead, or are we only playthings, inert as tin and long since dead? Can all this cascade of fevered meaning howling in every lover's breast, a trillion souls since the birth of all creation, really amount to naught, and merit no reply but its own negation? No answer comes from this high sky, unless rain be tears from some gargantuan being of whom we are the very thoughts that throng his head. Oh let it be so, that every tangent and trajectory, as vapour trails across the blue, is a thought, a life, the magnificent demise of me and you, as autumn dying in its hundred hues. We make such smoke as lasts a hundred years a piece, our lives the very music to make the angels weep.

*

A police station. By what perversion and degradation of common sense do I find myself crossing this threshold voluntarily? Verily I am by instinct no friend to the constabulary. But friend to Horace Stockbridge certainly, who saved me from the waves and let me catch my breath, nursed me back from the edge of death until my legs could bear my weight again. And as he healed my body, so have others catered for my soul, the dear Mustafa whose acquaintance I shall remake too before this moon is old. I am stronger in every way each day, while my fabled brother withers. Now take me to the pot in which they keep the snake so we can watch him slither.

The street our feet take us down is somewhat tumble-down. If the gentrified districts we crossed were smiles then this is more a frown. Façades all bashed in as old boxers' faces, bruised and ripped and stitched in places. Stucco weathered, peeled and patched. Thatched with moss and knotweed here and there, growing from the fissures spreading slowly everywhere. Render failing rather as human or reptilian skin: sorely used and growing rather thin. And due to shed perhaps some moment soon, a secret midnight or a sun-drenched noon when silence cloaks the expectant air like a she-spider waiting in her lair for the first clear word to bring her out to lunge and tear. Soon all will be revealed, is the message that I reach for, cloaked in metaphor, or is it fear? For so I sense and know, as something eerie tells me: here, I have been before.

We reach a door and pushing in find ourselves confronted with the habitual array of uniformed dunces at reception, too strapped for laughs to share a grin. Here one senses, time, patience and fresh air grown thin. *Good evening, officer...* Doctor Stockbridge clears his throat as to begin. *I have a letter here from a certain esteemed Swiss Doctor Schwitzer, I emailed it to you last week. Here's a copy, look, you'll have a record of it in your book...*

Dave! –the crew-cut jobsworth shouts as though addressing his desk, –*there's some bloke out here enquiring about a Vienna Schnitzel for his Bar Mitzvah, would you care to come and take a look?*

What, what? The eponymous Dave emerges from his backroom fug clutching a mug of slopping Horlicks to his bollocks in an expression of lopsided solipsism. Mouth twisted, he opines: *Des, Did you book those druggies and finish off those traffic fines?* Des shakes his head, whether in deft refusal or rueful despair we're left to make up our own minds. Dave turns to us. *Doctor Whatnot I believe?*

Stockbridge. And my understudy Nadir Renoir. I feel as if under study, as Dave considers me briefly like a slater exposed beneath a lifted rock, and turns his weary eyes skywards to the clock upon the time-stained wall.

I can spare five minutes with you right now, or not at all. He turns around abruptly as a sergeant major, our following him presumed to his luxurious and well-appointed room.

Excellent, officer. We can well appreciate your workload is heavy as your ability is small...

I nudge Horace. His newfound command of loquacious English is tenuous and dangerous. Such pride before a fall.

What's that? Dave half turns his head as he walks, a difficult operation for which he trained for years.

Availability. Stockbridge comes out of the tight corner, correcting himself adroitly if desperately. Dave listens uninterestedly. *Your availability. Your available time is small...*

Not at all. He smiles and sits behind his desk, indicating by the smallest inflexion that we should make ourselves at home. *I'm all ears...*

Well, as my email stated, on behalf of the esteemed Doctor Schwitzer, Interpol have granted me the authority by proxy to obtain certain files on one Thomas Leermouth, deceased. An unproven murder case which took place on this date here, see... Stockbridge tables the papers and punts them gamely across the table with all the filmic aplomb he can muster. *I am particularly interested in the addresses of the offences and those of the witnesses, the victims as alleged of Mister Leermouth's rather queer experiments.* Dave's eyebrows lift, the papers shift, one senses that he longs for a cigarette, or a suffragette to arrest, finding us quite the pest.

Here, says Dave at last, marking a few pages and firing aged rubber bands across the desk, *this is old shit now. I'll have Des photocopy these pages then you can be on your way. Was there any other business I can be doing for you today?*

As a matter of fact, I wonder if you might tell me which police station the artist Zenith Learmot is presently being held at. I read in the paper this morning that he has been charged with a fair barrage of villainy, after all these years of accumulating pillory from the very media whose praise his slithery...

I kick Stockbridge under the desk, anxious to curtail his inexpert verbiage.

Zenith, ah yes. Causing quite a stir over at Briarbarn Road I'm told, shouting promises of bribery through his prison bars, making frequent references and promises regarding his gold bars in Swiss bank accounts. But I don't think those will be worth much by the time he gets out. His goose is cooked, the way things look. Has this some connection with your Swiss professor?

Doctor.

Father confessor... I add irrelevantly, unable to restrain myself at last from the joy of a cheap rhyme, then stop in time from further indulgence.

Dave eyes me like a mouldy effulgence glimpsed on the dirty walls of his dreariest cells, marking me well. *Well?*

Only time will tell. Stockbridge brilliantly answers, resolving the situation with a clichéd collocation just in time. He goes up in my estimation. I've taught him well. And so we leave, the situation retrieved, reprieved, the gruff policeman deceived into thinking we are figures of credibility, unable to believe we've bluffed our stuff and taken personal information one ought not to disclose, in contradiction of all appropriate legislation, out from under his nose.

*

So, how to make use of our abuse of a policeman's trust? Phrased like that, 'tis quite a rare and unusual jewel we have in our hands as we wander about, the good doctor and I, strangers together in these strange lands. Inevitably enough, I want to go find my sordid sibling first, but Horace restrains me with an eminently logical refrain, somewhat wasted on my irrational brain: *To get to speak to Zenith behind bars may be no easy thing, requiring some extra special skulduggery and thuggery, bribery and imbibery, and if it goes wrong we'll be ejected from this noble region. Reasons are legion why we should press on with our more legal business first, culminating in the opening of your first artistic show tomorrow night. You'll want to meet with your friends beforehand, renew their acquaintance as they spray your canvases with fresh varnish and glue. I would if I were you. Thereafter, in the wake of much applause and laughter, you can slip out some tradesman's entrance to wreak all the revenge you like on your tyke of a brother.*

Revenge? I stop myself and him, slowing a little as we whittle our way through the woody streets, spring blossoms blowing at our feet, reaching a district a little more neat and complete. *Is that what you think is driving me still? Did I not speak of the love of a woman, of that urgency, that primordial thrill?* I find myself thinking of the words of Mustafa, sense my soul being weighed, as he conveyed, in some great scales above us tended by an unseen hand of infinite gentleness and wisdom.

I wonder though... Stockbridge ponders half to himself as we resume our stride, *if you'd be able to restrain yourself, given the unlikely opportunity to throttle and kill him. Those bars may prove a blessing, both for you and for him. The gap between them too thin to let him out, or to let you in.*

I laugh, grimly, answering his shrewdness with a grin, noticing that night is falling fast and that if this place has a public transport system then its mastery by tickets and timetables is a task too late for us to begin, today at least, I'm tired of being on my pins. Stockbridge treats me to a fine buffet dinner in a restaurant chosen on a whim, which fills as night goes on with loud Sylvians making a din. I get him drunk again and we spend the night in some bins. Chaste at least, in this place this time, with only rats to nibble on our extremities, no dubious saloon girls to quibble our moral proclivities. And a fine municipal fountain to shower in the next morning, what more could a fellow want? Stockbridge seems less than grateful, frightfully set in his ways and unable to adjust to the noble lifestyle I've perfected over so many years. I'm sure Mustafa understood and I resolve that I must discuss it with him again. Comfort and luxury are a terrible hindrance and corrosion of the mettle of men.

*

A new district then, and a strange trail to follow, astute and erect as bloodhounds, once at length I've found some coffee made of grounds of Herculean strength to throw down Stockbridge's throat. He glows at first like a ten pound bomb ready to explode then we're up and away and back on the road. Metronome men, we tick and tock, and talk at an accelerated rate as we confusedly follow a cheap tourist map, and I begin to get the queer notion that the café which sold me the coffee was not entirely kosher. *Amphetamine* sounds no more like coffee than sun tan lotion. Whatever the cause, the effect is much forward motion.

We arrive we think at our first address, and take some time to dust the excess of mess off each other's clothes while hiding behind a rose bush. An ambush, is what this feels like, poring over our photocopied details of a certain Gerald Meek, a lab technician who subjected himself to the alleged experiments of Thomas Leermouth in return for a hundred and fifty-six pounds a week. Cheap at the price I'd say, for the voyage of your life, back and forward in time, where's the crime? We hit the door chime and wait, wait a long time, for Meek's aged mother to shuffle to the door. She immediately seems all too ready to ignore us until we implore her to let us tell her son's story, in all its unsavoury glory, to an ignorant world, of all the untold harm that man Leermouth got to do before he was apprehended. *But how could they let him escape?* –she asks herself with a shake of her head while going to rouse Gerry himself from his bed. *That bastard doctor fair messed with his head.*

In time we hear the stairs creaking, and rambling sounds of speech leaking down from above, like the hoots of a wood dove nested in the world's eaves, or the laughter of God as he leaves us for the last time, tossing us the keys. Gerry Meek descends, his aged mother helping as his limbs bend, a travesty of the normal run of things for this man is not yet forty by the tally of mere years, according to our notes. Motes of dust spin in the morning sunlight from the seldom-parted curtains, a swirl of dishevelment about this sore sight on which our eyes alight. Long unkempt hair prematurely white, he sees us and recoils in fright: *The fumigator men, 'tis them again... back to flush the rats out of the basement and lick the mould from the walls like a whore's tongue on my balls, why are you always out, mother, when Dorothy Parker calls? It's not what I meant, what I meant at all, this clashing of rocks like unwashed socks at the charterhouse of dawn. You get me wrong? Then sing me a song to save me from the graceful faces of the men who mow the lawn. Their fingers are like knives impaling pale wives who run for their lives and sail off down the Ganges in washtubs made waterproof by mountaineering dubbing. Let's all go clubbing. The land-lubbing god who tied us to this clod of sod can answer at least for the dark mood of this flood and its constant thud against our hearts and heads as the tide rises. No surprises, you'll have it off with all that rubbing. Put a sock in it or a lampshade on it, stuff a flex up a poodle's arse and switch it like Christmas tree for you and me, one each in the abstract beach of snow where we meet before nobody goes. What direction is time? Primordial slime is the recurring terminus, looking up or down the line.*

What the devil is he talking about? −Stockbridge interjects in a sympathetic whisper into Mrs Meek's ear.

Oh, she says, almost smiling sadly, *he's been like this for years. Pay no attention to the generalities, they're invariably jumbled up, but the details sometimes mean things, well, half of them, and the other half are bollocks, pardon my French, gentlemen. Fumigator men for example, he's seeing them right now, as if you are them, but they came here five years ago and upset him because he had to vacate his room for two days. To him, this incident is real, still happening right now, he has no sense of time. His memories are not packed away, but constantly replaying, in an art gallery, permanently on display.*

Quick, Sir Nigel! Meek leaps to his feet and raises his hand as if hailing some passing dignitary. *Down by Whitman's Farm, the enemy are nigh! But what a roguish trouncing we might yet bring them too were we to be the better harriers this day...*

Ahh now this is his medieval phase. He sees knights riding through here apparently, something to do with the Wars Of The Roses, right across the living room. He often complains that I don't shovel the horse dung up from in front of the telly or that his feet are sliding on the cobbles, but our living room is fitted carpet as you can both see. Oh deary me. I've grown quite used to all this I'm afraid, strange and harrowing to you as it undoubtedly might be. Can I get you both a cup of tea?

When Mrs Meek goes to leave the room, Stockbridge gets up and sits beside Meek on the settee, passing a hand in front of his eyes as the man goes on muttering. *Mr Meek, Gerald... Gerry... can you hear my voice, are you aware of the two of us, two visitors sitting in the living room with you? Do you know where you are? Sitting in your living room at home? Can you see us?*

I hear you... the voice replies at last, tired and cracked, as if from far away through layer upon layer of quilts, a man deeply asleep or imprisoned beneath the weight of his own eyelids. *What seekest thou in this land? I have more motives for men than hats and gloves, but none for you to hand.*

Did you know a Doctor Thomas Leermouth twenty years ago? Did he harm you in some way...?

Phhhhhh... Meek lets out a violent expulsion of air, purses his lips then paces about the room with disturbing velocity then bangs his head into the fireplace wall. His mother returns holding the tea pot high in her hands and as she pauses in the door for a moment, Meek lets out a deep guttural animal wail then grabs the poker from beside the fireplace and runs with it flailing around his head and swings it majestically as Excalibur into the teapot's side with an almighty boom, sending it skidding and spilling right across the room.

Stockbridge and I seem a good deal more shocked than Mrs Meek who takes it all somewhat philosophically and decidedly in her stride, returning to her kitchen to fetch a bucket and cloth, while the doctor and I restrain her son on the sofa as his mouth pours with froth.

What? What heresy didst thou quoth? Leermouth stuck me in the goalmouth then aimed a thousand bladders at my nuts. Penalty time. Sick to the death and walloped in the guts. Guinea pig served raw I was with mighty sore baws. A fiery little homunculi fetched out of the foundry with red-hot glowing hammer and tongs. Ah the voices voiceless that throng my hiddenness. It was he that opened up the hatch in my head, set a batch of twelve-inch singles playing on my turntable then left me there for dead. Ahh, ah'm fair fucked lads, it's time we packed me off to bed.

As Meek quietens down, Stockbridge goes to help his mother with the mop and broom and I feel some idiotic obligation to break the silence in the room. *How did he do it, this experiment? Drugs, hallucinations and suggestions?*

Meek breathes a long rasping noise, harrowing and horrible and I suddenly become terrified that I have been left alone in the room with him. *It's you!* He screams aloud, scrabbling backwards on the sofa, crab-like, his eyes staring unseeing, roaming wildly across the room. *That voice! Keep your paws off my hair, it's all growed back so you can't touch me anymore. How did you find me, you fiend!? I'd sooner have had leukaemia than this temporal anaemia. You wicked emissary of perverted academia. Call this toxic intoxication life then I'd sooner choose abstemia!* And with that he takes one last run and launches himself headfirst straight through the living room window.

*

That went well... I reflect to Stockbridge, as we hasten away from Meek's tearful mother, the ambulance doors closing behind her son. *A good morning's work done.*

He'll be fine... the good doctor muses, *–just a few bruises and flesh wounds. His mother seemed to think it was time they took him in for review anyhow. And we swept all the glass up nicely didn't we? It should be making eye-catching ballast in her shrubbery by now. What did you say to him though? I caught only a snatch of it while I was fetching a new batch of Hoover bags. You seemed to send him right over the edge, and indeed the hedge and the petunias.*

Loony logic as only a loony has. And come to think of it, the moon is full today and will hold full sway across a regal night too soon if we go on squandering our wanderings to expedite your theories in this way.

Nithna... Stockbridge turns to look at me as we pace down leafy noonday streets again, *If I didn't know you better I'd swear you were trying to change the subject or indeed the sport to some game that you were better placed to play. Could that fellow have recognised you with his wrecked eyes, even though you've been through a face or two?*

I doubt it seriously, don't you? The present seemed to make less impact on him than the price of oil in Timbuktu.

Indeed, or 1462. I suppose you'll be contemplating consulting a library to see what historical realities he was viewing with his psychic telescope.

No need. I could see the man was quite deranged, estranged from reality, in actuality. Let us give our attention to the neglected sport of punctuality.

*

So in time we come to a yet sadder clime, a melancholy bungalow amid an avenue of limes. And more and more now in Sylvia I find my feet and mind atremble as fragments of vistas resemble memories all jumbled up and pushed away out of sight in my cognitive attic. Does Horace Stockbridge know I'm at it? –Pretending to him that I am in all respects a mental white sheet, when in fact I am gaining unwelcome self-knowledge with every sorry street? Who can we trust on this earth? A dearth of friends is what the truly honest man would all too quickly find, were such a fool creature to exist upon this world. Oh yes, remind me, there was one once, and they crucified him for his trouble. Or a wise man, yes, of genuine and total perspicacity and sagacity, I wonder if he would have much taste or capacity for friends and time among his fellow men, when every second he could see their writhing thoughts recoiling and contriving to bend each other to their ends. I put my hands up to my dishevelled hair and am amazed to realise how much time has idled by since I last used the rusting wires concealed there. With a kind of panic I part the buttons of my tunic to make sure the dial upon my chest is still extant and has not been stolen by some harlot or footpad who caught me unawares. I sigh with relief. It's there, it's there. But why do I care? I seem not to have made much use of it of late. Do my otherworldly powers at last abate?

We ring the doorbell, and in a while a middle-aged man stands there puzzling at us in the bright light of afternoon, and cordially invites us in to talk and soon we find we three are freely discussing the lost life of his late wife Rachel Blackwell. He makes us tea and leads us to his study, ushering us to sit opposite him on a large leather settee. The house is modest but drab, with an air of something indefinably sad and male, the absence of a woman's touch, somehow cold and pale. He has not re-married, and photographs of her lovely face are scattered about the place amid, atop, tasteful hardwood shelves and armoires draped with Turkish cloths. A grandfather clock ticktocks somewhere in an echoing hall, and dust feels just a little too undisturbed in this solitary future whose occupant given the choice, one senses, would not have chosen this at all.

Blackwell begins: *Rachel and he, Professor Leermouth, they became friends you see, quite close for a while, sometimes I even wondered if there might have been something between them, the way she talked about him, but she always denied that. Him a neuro-scientist, her still an impressionable student. He exploited her you see, her trust, the rat. At first she was just a volunteer, imagine that. That's how enthralled she was to his appalling theories.*

What were his experiments? Stockbridge prompts compassionately, stirring his tea.

Well, she signed a secrecy agreement, I wasn't supposed to be told anything, but Rachel, bless her, extended that circle of confidence to secretly include me. But was that any blessing, I wonder? Well at least I knew, know, why she died and who was responsible. It was all about hypnotic retrogression. Most scientists dismiss it, excommunicate any heretics who dare to even sniff at the supernatural. But he was shrewd and careful. Had been quietly going to performances and interviewing practitioners for years, befriended a few, got them to teach him the basic techniques. It's not like swinging a pocket watch and 'are you feeling sleepy?" you know, that's all just popular myth stage show stuff, it can be done with more subtlety and control than that, so Rachel reported. Leermouth started practising it himself, on a few subjects, Rachel and some others, sworn to secrecy. Said he'd taken them back to their childhoods, that sort of thing. But he'd invented this gizmo, "the hairnet" Rachel used to call it. A grid of wires and sensors he fitted over the head of the hypnotised subject, used it to measure exactly the electric field patterns of the brain. But it wasn't just a measuring device, it was an inducer. He didn't need to hypnotise anyone anymore you see, after the first session to map their brain. He just turned the dial up, induced the same currents again in their brain and they went to sleep and started voyaging through their own memories.

At this point, Doctor Stockbridge is unable to resist casting a glance over at me, with eyebrow raised, his face animated with fascination. Blackwell continues: *But according to Rachel things got stranger after that. Leermouth discovered that if he kept going with subjects, right back to their birth, they could go beyond, they would find themselves inside the body of another person, someone who had lived before in a previous generation.*

Reincarnation?

Yes, ridiculous isn't it? He had film recordings he showed Rachel apparently, of what she had said under hypnosis, speaking in strange accents and archaic languages, that sort of thing.

How far did he claim to be able to take her back? —I ask now, unable to maintain my restrained composure in the face of such mysterious disclosure. James Blackwell looks towards me curiously, his eyes unfocussed, his mind far away.

Oh... way back. The middle ages, then even before the Romans. Crazy stuff. Rachel said they verified some of it, or tried to. Historical maps confirmed the location of some cotton mill she had "relived", that was the term they invented, not "remember". She had relived being a woman working in a cotton mill, and they found the site and supposedly neither Rachel nor Leermouth could have known its existence beforehand. But they would have said that, wouldn't they? Perhaps it was all baloney. Oh yes, and other things, an ancient fort, a stockade built in the water somewhere in some remote loch. They drove away there together one weekend, which I wasn't happy about... maybe the whole thing was just a cover for him hitting on her. But of course they claimed they found the landmarks she had seen in her "reliving"... lost standing stones buried in the peat up to their tips, not marked on any map, ancient stepping stones under the water in a pattern you could run across at speed if you memorised them, but which outsiders and attackers would never master. It was utter madness. I felt I was beginning to lose her by then, as if she was coming under that man's spell, like a warlock.

Did you ever meet him? –I ask, with no inconsiderable trepidation.

Again, that turn of the head, and the slightly startled look from Blackwell. *No... strangely enough, although I tried to. Tried to ask questions at the university he was attached to, to launch a complaint against him if necessary, although I didn't want to make trouble for Rachel, just to try and extricate her from his spell. I think I saw him once at a distance getting into his little yellow sports car, but he drove off at speed. He had longish dark hair turning white, an ageing hippie, you know the type. Do you know he got Rachel to shave all the hair off her head? All her lovely long blonde locks. She cut it all off for him and she wore wigs instead, like she was a flaming cancer patient. Just so his 'hairnet" would work better on her. Can you imagine how I felt about that? She said it was worth it for the money he was paying her for the experiment sessions, but I couldn't see that anything was worth that. I don't think it was about money after a while anyway. She believed it all, and believed in him and wanted to find out how it would all end. We disagreed and argued about it a lot, began to fight.*

What did happen in the end?

Leermouth said he wanted to go public with his results, that there might even be big money in it one day, a company selling voyages into past lives, "Heredyssey" he planned to call it, hereditary odyssey, he probably even registered a domain name. But before that he said he needed to test his "Forward Hypotheses".

What did that mean?

He discovered he could reverse some of the currents in the brain patterns and induce the subject to go forward.

Forward?

Yes, so if Rachel was in the 18th century and he wanted to bring her forward to the 19th, he turned a dial. But of course, the question occurred to him after a while: what would happen if he kept her going forward to the present day then beyond? Into the future in other words.

Did that work?

Blackwell shrugs his shoulders. *It was probably all hogwash. But she believed it apparently.*

What did she, or he, see?

She would never tell me. But a look of pain and terror entered her eyes that day, that never left her until she died. She came home shaking and crying, a nervous wreck. She said she'd seen the future, ours and mine, and that it was better not to know, that nobody in fact, nobody should ever want to know the future, that it was the worst kind of curse imaginable to have that knowledge. She said she wanted to lose her memory, to be lobotomised even. She started drinking heavily, taking pills to get to sleep. Leermouth destroyed her, whatever it was he did, whatever it was he convinced her that she'd seen. And that's how she died you know… a cocktail of prescription drugs, as they said. A cocktail… doesn't that sound chirpy? –Like a wild party. But she was so alone towards the end, inside her head, no matter how I or anyone else tried, you couldn't reach her. She didn't even leave a suicide note. I don't suppose she needed to. Her life had become a suicide note, our every conversation, for the final few weeks.

I'm sorry for your loss, Mister Blackwell. Stockbridge says at last after an appropriate silence.

Oh? So was he apparently, Leermouth. Tended to confirm my theory that something had been going on, or that he'd had a crush on Rachel at least, unrequited, an older man and a beautiful young woman. Or maybe I'm being unfair. Maybe it was remorse for what he'd done. But he phoned here repeatedly, in distress, wanted to come to the funeral, but I told him I'd break his legs if he came anywhere near. He began sobbing like a child down the phone. I told him I had told the police what I knew about his experiments and that he should expect a knock on the door soon. That seemed to shut him up. I heard he went on the run after that… and well, you probably know the story, he shot himself. But tell you what… I remember something else he said on the phone, maybe the last thing he ever said to me. He said he was going to "go back and change things". Maybe he just meant trash his lab and destroy the evidence, or maybe something else, something weirder to do with all his creepy ideas about time and memories. I suppose he changed the future at least, for the better, by removing himself from it. Maybe we should all be grateful for that, one fragment of redemption. I don't think I've ever wished anyone's death. But the news of his, after everything, God forgive me, was a relief.

Thank you, Mister Blackwell, for sharing all that with us. I realise the memories must be painful, even after all these years... As Stockbridge talks, I find I have stood up, bewitched as in a trance and danced across the room to face into the photo-portrait of Rachel above the mantelpiece, her eyes like dark tunnels into which my consciousness funnels, slips and trips and drips in runnels.

The police closed the case a long time ago, how come someone's interested in this again? —I dimly hear Blackwell asking, as if he is a hundred miles away across a sea of spray.

My colleague, the esteemed Swiss Doctor Erno Schwitzer believes he has a patient with memory loss who may have been involved with Leermouth, is showing similar symptoms to those you have so kindly and helpfully recounted to us as Rachel's. The man is very ill apparently, mentally, and any kind of light on his history could be most revealing.

Then I am glad to have been of some assistance. There was some sensationalist news coverage at the time of course, but after that people lost interest. It hurts me sometimes to think that Rachel has been forgotten.

Oh, but she is not forgotten. I find myself saying, as the two of us stand to leave, not quite able to believe the unbidden words slipping from my mouth, as we shake hands with Blackwell. Stockbridge looks at me askance, aghast, then retrieves the save like an expert goalie, quelling an advance. *You keep her memory eloquently alive, Mister Blackwell... and now you've shared it with us also, for which we are most grateful.* Slowly, and wholly chastened we depart that holy shrine to lost love and time, wherein a flame endures to whose poignancy none but the hardest heart could be inured.

*

Now the afternoon hurries on, the light grows weary... we must go see your friends and seize your new destiny as a talked-about painter whose fortunes are on the rise. –I hear Stockbridge say this by my side as we stroll, but I am still miles away as the roll of thunder on a distant horizon. I am in strange turmoil, and if pressed could not attest as to what constituent parts my conflicting thoughts comprise.

You know, the good Doctor takes my arm, *I am alarmed as to how quiet you've become today, and odder still I'd say you've even started rhyming less, that might be significant, but quite of what I cannot guess.*

Bless you, Doctor, for your concern, but I believe my ailment is no more mysterious, and indeed no less, than what is customarily called Déjà vu. Perhaps my alleged new status as an artistic parvenu will do the trick to lift the gloom and restore some conversational hilarity between me and you.

Could you be Leermouth? Stockbridge punts the awful question, the looming chasm, intimidating phantasm, then throws me a lifeline to quell my spasms, *–or one of his other victims perhaps, of whom we know there were a few, not all of which the police ever found to speak to?*

I know not, I sigh, *I have forgotten, as was perhaps that poor girl's desire, all regret and epithet of years past apt to make me sad or tire.* And only to the present now or future, can my heart aspire. I am drawn forwards as by angels singing to whatever revelation awaits me next, in punishment or recompense, my task to shed one final mask.

*

So I only had to ask. Or disappear, dispense with fear. Now here I am at last outside an art gallery solely dedicated to my work, I can't believe my luck. Look, there is my name (or one of them at least) proclaimed across the launch-night banners. I stammer as I cross the threshold, full of disbelief. T'would almost be relief to find it all an error, the mouse in me recoils in terror. But there they are, straight up ahead: canvases and pastels I recognise as mine, strange and yet familiar, glimpsed dimly from some other time. And Mustafa and Kettering, muttering in a back room, catch sight of me and come running out, overjoyed: *Ithir! What miracle is this? We all feared you drowned or dead!*

Indeed! We lock in a tri-partite embrace, nearly bang our heads. *It is as if I have been dead and now return to mourn at my own burial.*

Much better than that by far, you silly old goat! Here, let me take you by the hand and throat, and squeeze the life half out you to check all's real about you. –Kettering exclaims, until we descend to calling each other disrespectful names, as was our habitual game of old. *Dirty gypsy bastard, old dead-beat rock-and-roller,* we laugh and holler.

You have changed I see, old friend... Mustafa marvels, *and writ upon your face are all your travels. In fact, hold on, the very shape of your nose and brow, the colour of your eyes. How can this be? –Your soul re-housed in a vessel of a different shape and size?*

I cannot understand it either, and have learned it's better not to even try. Besides, after a drink or ten, who truly recollects the face of men? 'Tis our spirit and our voices about tonight we should be rejoicing. I did not know I had done so many oils, how noble of you to build such a monument of the spoils of my abscondment. And what uncanny luck that I should chance upon you in this arrondissement. Here, in fact, how could I forget? –I owe this very meeting to this friend here patiently waiting throughout this greeting, Doctor Horace Stockbridge.

More hands are shaken as the doctor joins the group, bottles cracked open, everybody cock-a-hoop. The wine and stories flow and bit by bit my spirits take to the air, as standing by the stair I dimly register the first guests entering then more thereafter, much hilarity and laughter. My private view, my vernissage, parvenu and ingénue, my soirée a la carte and sur le plage. Premier étage. But oh, behind this visage, how my soaring spirits turn like an eagle and venture out too far and high into my own sky and by and by I find myself more distant than I would have planned or desired. All the voices and faces turn to one, one vast auditory hallucinatory hum, a cacophonic choir. I find myself drawn, glass in hand, to stand before my own pictures puzzling over their deeper meanings. It is as if I hear a bird cry, plaintively keening, something lost, a knife-sharp fragment of returning meaning. Every face on each canvas bears some resemblance to Rachel Blackwell, or is it to some other woman looming in memory or obsession? –Cynthia, Gladys, or my brother's Aphrodite, on whose trail I'd rather be tonight if I were half so drunk and twice as sprightly? And figures lying on chairs without their hair, and nets across their faces fixed in sleeping grimaces, and everywhere symbols scattered as if plundered out of shopping trips through history. Crosses, swastikas, runes and Sanskrit interweaved in symbolist mysteries older than time and maybe older, someone is talking at my shoulder. Kettering, whittering, he's reading my thoughts like psychic join-the-dots, or has been creating them, weaving them with his own verbosity, like hypno retro gresso-whatzity:

Who was that girl who was all over you at the end of that show in Oceania on that last occasion? I last saw the two of you vanish into that goodnight together, arm in arm for all the world as if you'd been like that forever and all set to sail off down the river. Then bang! There was noise, confusion, gunshots even, you were banished, leaving. Famished for news we've been since. What did it mean can you evince? That bold stramash so close to the Feast of Stephen.

They took her… I mumble… the sharp-toothed rats… my brother's orthodontic rodents, I should have seen the portents… but no fear I'm on the trail and won't fail to find her, or if you find her first please do remind her… I say from behind my haze, gazing into a glazed bottle and emptying its contents.

And next, minutes or hours gone by, its hard to say, I find Mustafa at my side, painting pictures in my ear with his melodic brush of words. *It is good to see you my friend, but consider if you would, our mutual acquaintance Kettering as he is stood there at the other side of the room, entertaining what company he can about him gather…*

What about the good fellow? I ask, blurry.

Consider how little jealousy he feels towards you, although this is your show and not his, and your paintings are selling like proverbial hot bagels. You're getting praise and acclaim tonight of a level which he has craved for years. And yet, I see only joy in his heart on your behalf. A man cannot fake such light-heartedness, such a smile and such a laugh.

Yes, that is good. I admire the man, but I'm not sure I grasp your point entirely...

As ever, Ithir, this is about you and your brother. Would you feel so little jealousy towards Kettering were the roles reversed? —And did you, when he was flourishing and you were but his assistant, his under-study, factotum, back in Oceania? You see, you are well-rehearsed in negative emotions. But didn't I tell you once how your soul is being weighed? Or was my point too subtle, or the metaphor flawed by which it was conveyed? You are fond of asking what the point is of all this game, and yet perhaps you have been told the truth already but simply did not recognise its name.

Mustafa... I have changed already under your teaching, altered as clay by a potter's hand. And you must know I seek a woman now, love itself, whom I have glimpsed, a fragment fallen from heaven. Is that not proof enough that I have honed my arrow towards the holy straight and narrow?

Ithir. This whole word is but a construct, a stage play in which even I am merely scenery devised to test your soul. So it is for every man and woman as they strain their eyes, crossing fog-clogged bogs to seek their prize. Never mistake life for being real. Only the soul must be your goal. To cleanse it and find truth, to face everything, each charge, each crime, each indictment, and tally up the balance-sheet of your own folly. To unlock the magic box in which we're trapped and be released into enlightenment; the trick is not to win out over others at all, but to lose beautifully. Your greatest painting, your ultimate work of art, is your self, and suffering your only brush, the only thing to make your colours lush. You must renounce hatred and jealousy before you can complete your odyssey...

*

And so these words, out of so many echoing others, become the ones that assail my waking state the next day, well after noon, in some luxurious boarding-house my kind friends must have booked me into, using all my fresh windfall funds from spectacular sales. A knocking on the door is waking me, and rising unsteadily I let Doctor Horace in. *Are you fresh and rested Nithna?*

I nod my head. *Something close, a few stops up from dead. Have we a mission today? —I feel something of that ilk slopping round my head.*

Indeed. We go directly to jail without passing go, I believe, although there are a couple of other locales within my notes into which we could have poked our noses if our reposes had but ended sooner.

Like?

Thomas Leermouth's former home, a ruin now I believe, as grandiose and mysterious as Rome.

And all roads have been leading there, is that it?

Not quite the carrot for you as your brother and his ingénue, unless your priorities are changing. Its time you put an end to your estrangement, him and you, lest all this friction end in your derangement.

I thought I started out mad and ill in your estimation, or have I misunderstood the arrangement?

Whatever. You've reminded me of something your friend Mustafa said last night. Deep fellow that. Something about time only being comprehensible when we remove its vector. He's expecting to see us again tonight, I hope you're not planning on doing anything unsightly today at the police station to get us expelled or extradited?

I only want to get my business expedited. A name, a location, for my new flame. I must trace her before I forget her face.

Very well. Let's go. I'll show, you tell, if you promise to quell your anger well.

*

Another constabulary. Describing it would involve invective and diminutives fit to exhaust even my vocabulary. Drab and drear and dreich, and full to the brim with the uniformed uninformed, who fill out forms ad infinitum. Dear Doctor Horace does his bit, chatty patter to butter up the batty copper in charge, congratulating him for not leaving the dreaded Zenith Learmot at large. And could we interview him as part of our study, cue the ridiculous Swiss aside, believing he has had some contact with our unnamed amnesic patient.

Truth be told I feel exultant, triumphant and ancient, being led into the room in which my brother faces me at last through iron bars. *I can unlock these gates,* the superintendent offers, *if I lock the outer doors instead.*

Please... Horace snorts, *do not put ideas into our head. Better to keep him at a distance in this instance.*

Whatever, Plod shrugs, *I'll leave the keys beside the chair, now I'll go get out your hair.*

Silence descends as Zenith wakens stiffly from his thin foam mattress on the floor, and glances over us and behind us sees the gently closing door. *Brother, I've been expecting you. Does it please you now to see our fortunes so reversed at last?* His smile makes me flinch. The power of his personality, his apparent magnanimity shakes me somehow like a psychic strip search. *Who is this clown you've brought with you?*

Doctor Horace Stockbridge, sir, at your service. The good doctor steps forward and thrust his hand through the bars.

Zenith laughs aloud. *Your personal shrink! How very quaint.* Without warning he takes and twists Stockbridge's hand round rapidly, thrusts another hand through the bars around his throat and strangles him expertly until he faints, then lets him slump to the floor. I stumble back in horror, frozen in inactivity, falling backwards onto a seat. The keys... my mind races, are still over by the door. Zenith's eyes follow mine minutely, reading me. *That's right,* he smiles, sweating, exulting. *Your every thought is known to me, brother. You can't hide your weakness and cowardice from me, even here in a city of so many trees to duck behind. Your triumph doesn't taste so sweet does it? Revenge tastes empty in your mouth, because really you wish you were me, wish you had my audacity and strength. You don't want to kill me or crush me at all, or whatever snivelling fantasy you've been harbouring half your life. You want to become me, but you can't because you lack the balls. We're like man and wife, you and I. Different but contrapuntal, yin and yang. Come on, come over here and strangle me. Prove to yourself and me that you know how to kill, that you're up to the challenge. Then maybe, just maybe, you'll be worthy, you can call yourself cruel and brutal enough to harbour my appetites, to exact and realise your will. That's what success is, brother, a triumph of the will. Because most people out there, ninety-nine percent, are little sheep, waiting for a shepherd, good or bad they can't tell the difference, someone with all the decisiveness and willpower which they sense they lack. You see, the good lord in his wisdom doesn't seem to have handed out much initiative and leadership. They're in mighty short supply. And mighty indeed are those who realise that and cultivate it. And wanna know the most self-empowering and decisive act of all? To kill! To kill, brother! To defy life itself...*

Zenith kneels and begins to twist Horace's neck and I panic, run towards the door to raise the alarm, but Zenith rasps: *Stop! Bring me the keys over or I'll break his neck. Can't you hear it clicking already? Just another few notches round and you'll hear the lovely sound, a fatal weakness in the human design, this narrow vulnerable canal to the brain through which everything must flow. Death is almost instant I'm told, from a relatively simple blow.*

I pick up the keys and find I am walking back slowly, like a zombie, a damned puppet working to his command. I feel the edges of the keys with my sweating slippery hands, their edges and serrations, their points and tips. Approaching suddenly I lunge and thrust the sharpest with all the force of my body behind it, straight into his throat. Aiming for the jugular, whoever taught him anatomy it seems, taught us both.

Hiss and froth of blood in blinding spray across my eyes. Letting go of Stockbridge, Zenith's grabbing me instead and smashing me against the bars with terrifying force, trying to crack my skull or crack the gate. Making hideous hissing sounds now, he's reaching for his face to remove the keys. Both of us slick with blood I try to beat him to it and our hands interlock, fingers interweave about the keys. *Tell me,* I say, *who the girl was, her name and where she is, where to find her...*

What girl? –He rasps grotesquely, spraying blood like a fatal lisp.

The one I got talking to in Oceania, before your thugs took her away, long brown hair, blue eyes, said she was from Sylvia originally... tell me.

Zenith has the upper hand on the keys now, although his strength is fading. *Thea...* he says... *her name is Thea, you'll find her in Suburbia... if you hurry.*

Hurry? Suddenly he punches me hard in the face and I recoil violently across the room, the back of my head striking the wall. I nearly black out for a second, and when I open my eyes, incredibly, the cell behind the bars is empty. I stand up and stagger forward, thinking perhaps Zenith is on the floor, hidden by the slumped form of Doctor Stockbridge, but there's nobody there. I look down at my hands, covered in blood and see that, stained very red and almost unrecognisable in the midst of my palm: I still hold the keys. I go over to the gate and check the lock but it's not been opened. Confused, reeling, heart still racing but sensing some kind of peculiar release and freedom, I kneel and take Horace's pulse. He's still breathing.

Stepping away backwards slowly, dumfounded, disbelieving, I reach the door and turn the handle. And leave, leave. Walk then run and run until I can scarcely breathe. Blocks away I collapse into some green copse, streaked with sweat. But to kill one's self is not so easy, I'm breathing yet. But am I dreaming or has there been some change? Deranged beneath the beating sun, it seems my dual has been murdered by our duel. The jewel I clutch in my hand: blood-red, is better than any diamond or ruby, the key which I have won. I am no longer twin it seems, but one.

~

PART

FIVE

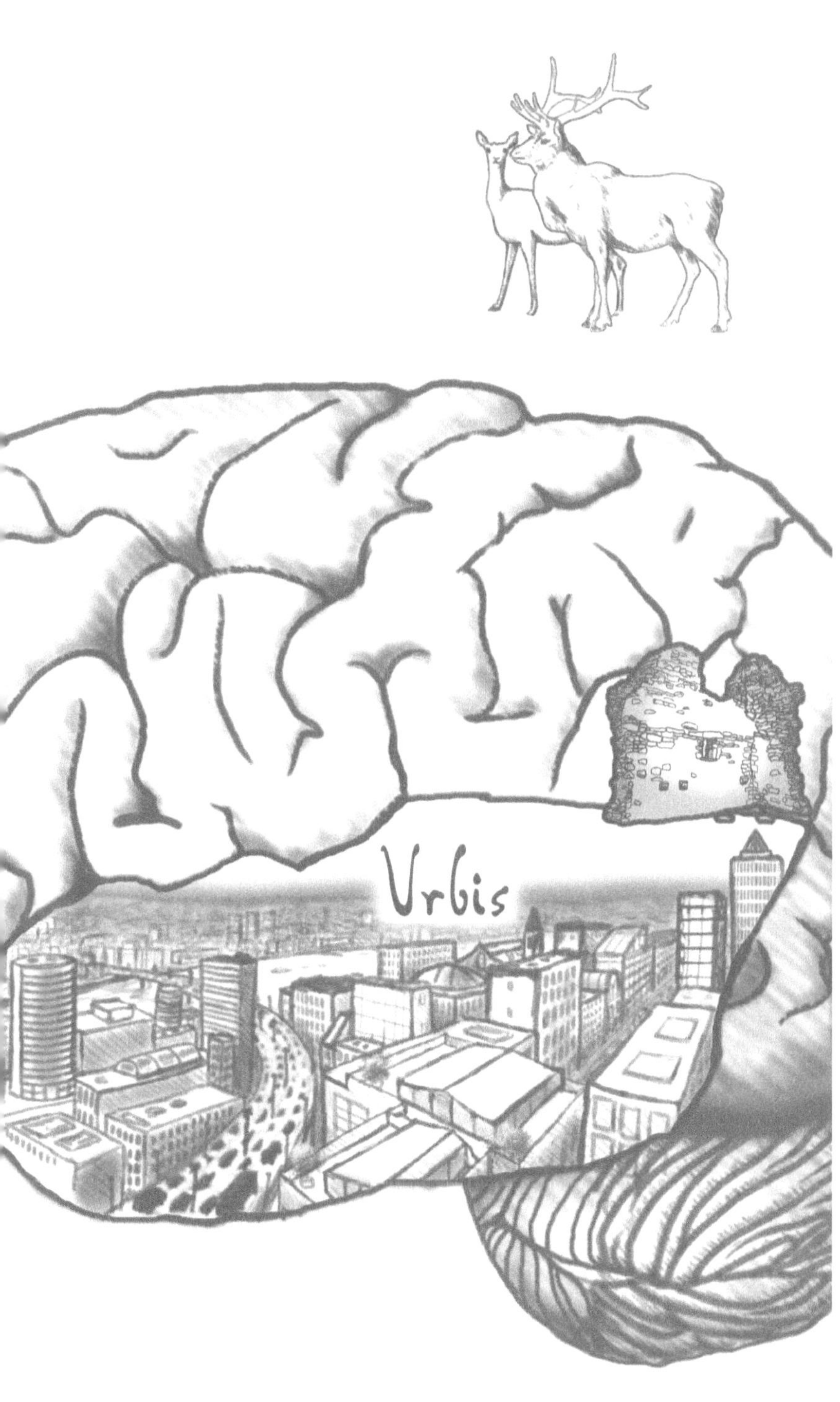
Urbis

So as melancholy darkness falls once more in the town of trees, I make my way I know not where, guided as by my feet on rails. Horror, guilt, still lurches in my entrails, but exhilaration, exultation also pumps my blood, with all that that entails. I have triumphed somehow, or taken off some blindfold and walked out clearly into truth. Or nearly, so I feel, for as darkness falls so also a veil is lifting, all my perspectives shifting. I begin to recognise all the landmarks around me, to walk with greater purpose than before. I turn corners with confidence and each time spot a building here and there that seems different, has been replaced at some indeterminate date, but know not how I come by this knowledge.

Things get darker and my heart lurches. I pass two churches that I sense once told me I was nearly home. Then here at last I chance upon what Horace described to me as Rome. A large ruined house behind demolition fencing, brooding dark and pensive. Interspersed with many trees self-sown and grown wild for twenty years. Tall cypresses and junipers weave in and out of broken window casements, thick roots of ivy sprout from cracking walls. Collapsed roofs undulate in seas of broken tiles, through which umbrella pines soar in artistic poses languid and wind-torn, lovelorn and forlorn. Grave-like guarding dead dreams in eternal hope of dawn. The rain is on now, and drips like tears from the eaves, and a few leaves alike, in a slow fountain of picturesque decay and degradation, falling, follow suit. Is summer getting tired already, chastened, hastened by autumn's pursuit?

I steal through a gap in the fence torn by miscreant children or foxes, and climb a wall or two, then go in through a window. My mind's eye flashes every so often like neurons firing, phantom glimpses in vision's periphery of how this house was once, before time's sly intrusion and derision, debased it, exposed, as by a surgeon's cruel incision. Painted plaster fragments on wall, glimmers of smashed glass, crumpling fans of delaminating lath. Fungus of rot and sprays of graffiti proclaiming gang rites. Discarded needles, condoms, and tights. Oh the delights of forbidden forgotten places. Children, adolescents, villains. I can almost see their faces, even without my wires to dangle. Then I come to the place where all confusion untangles.

Once a study at the back of my house, the floor's centre is commanded by a rotting old couch, its stuffing lanced and thrown hither to the wind's fey dance. But there are lockers here and safes, which though rusting have proven too heavy to give up their place in two long decades. Nor indeed their secrets. And I alone know where the keys have languished. Reaching my hands under rotten shelves I nearly think all is lost and taste my panic. Then at last, my fingers stop and repeat, as reading Braille in disbelief. I bend down and retrieve a little key, miraculously dry and uneroded, protected by the work of spiders.

Then by the moon's light now rising above the windowless shards of a façade like a heartbroken face, I unfold a sparkling net of electrodes, a jiggling jellyfish of twilight stars, and lift it to my head with slow ceremony as a priest donning his vestments, a judge preparing to pass sentence. And the lab pack and the dials, the vials of chloroform, and even batteries. All are here and safe and dry and their time has come at last as I lie and sink into the rotting scum of soaking cushions, and throw my head back and reach for the dial… and turn. And turn.

The house comes alive briefly in an explosion of light, a soft effulgence of grace pouring over my face and burning out my features. The wound on the back of my head, the ache in my heart, time heals all sutures, as walls rebuild themselves, stones lifting magically into the air like birds to take their rightful places in walls. I am shot, not into the future, but deep then deeper into the past, in fact perhaps whatever destination my equipment took me last.

Twilight again. A world seen dimly as through a haze of deepest cobalt blue. I wear strange attire of tights and belted tunic and cloak, walking through corridors of dark carved wood. I am quite well-to-do, some sort of count or prince. I walk out onto the battlements of my tower, and look all around me with an exultant glower. A beautiful wide coastline spreads before me looking north, somehow familiar but changed, simple land of peasants undisfigured by industry. My pastime is to gaze into the future, suitably inspired and deranged by nefarious substances procured for me secretly by a local witch who I had spared from the bonfire in return for her services, a clandestine apothecary. I write down prophecies upon wide rolls of parchment with a feather pen, a quill is what I will call it. For a bed I have a four poster carved for my grandfather, shot through with little holes of woodworm. The roof beams click at certain times of year with death-watch beetle. For a toilet I use a hole in the wall, discharging straight out towards the grass surrounding embankments below, chilly in winter.

I am laird over all the surrounding lands. Vassals come to greet me, pledging fealty and I reassure them, gripping both their hands. And from still further occasionally, indeed across all the known country and even across the seas, curious visitors come to hear me speak and discuss with me the substance of what I have spoken before. And here is what's important, since some can neither read nor write, to help them memorise my words: I speak in rhyme.

I wake suddenly with a terrible jolt. Faces about me in the twilight ruins all look down laughing and shouting, deranged in firelight, a gang of little demons. One of them swings a piece of wood with several nails protruding from it towards my head and I cower in fear, protecting myself with one hand, but with the other: turn the dial again in panic. Groan…moan… heaving of machinery whining, idling, struggling, breaking down, its work beginning then failing, damaged or incomplete.

I stand up and dust myself off. I am in the ruins of the old house again. I reach up and find the hairnet has caught fire and fused itself onto my scalp. I reach my hand down onto my breast, and again some intense heat has caused a small explosion that has severely burnt my chest. The dial is fused. And yet I feel no pain. Indeed I feel quite light-headed, sprightly. Night has lifted somehow, though I can think of no way to judge how much time has passed. Dawn now licks around the horizon, an early morning, the first perhaps of summer. I remember only one thing of importance: that I must head north and as fast as possible, to find Thea, my Aphrodite, where she reputedly resides in Suburbia. I remember, from what feels like many years ago, the map my friend Weasel drew me in chalk upon a wall. The quickest route to Suburbia is due north through Urbis, the peculiar centre which unvisited, has until now haunted my every distant horizon like a recurring dream, while somehow always remaining unimagined and unreal. Before the sun comes up too far and streets begin to throng and someone apprehends me for all the things I have done wrong, I must away with haste. I am Nadir in this place, so let us leave it, and leave behind my face.

*

Then in time to the border twixt Sylvia and Urbis I come, marked by a distinct diminution in the abundance, not of buildings, but of trees. We are heading inwards you see, towards the conurbation, the great conflagration of a million hearts and minds, hastening together in doubt and loneliness and eagerness as to what they'll find. Towerblocks. Neon nocturnal mirrors flicking on and off throughout long nights, that offer back vistas of yellow portholes with faces at them, searching and lost as ourselves. Are we wanted, are we desired? Are we discarded, left upon the shelves? What is it we seek to sell each other in this vast Halloween ball of a power-cut supermarket, polythene bags over our heads? Suffocating for attention, miming SOS? Or simply suffocating, trying to save the mess. Is loneliness the burden or the prize? Is hell ourselves or all the rest, everybody else, closing their eyes?

I am in the thick of it now. A real city rises up around me with its inhabited cliffs. Huge interchanges and bypasses behave irrationally, trying to confuse my feet, throw off the humble pedestrians like ticks from their writhing serpentine skin, black and shiny, slithery in sodium and halogen light. Why is morning so paused and delayed? Does pollution haze this domain so thickly that even sunlight and happiness cannot penetrate its glaucous depths? The roads are still quiet, so I take to their middle when the pavements get obstreperous with me. I begin to remember landmarks with surprising clarity. Visual cues bringing memories like bells ringing through the fog. I am heading home suddenly, legs trotting, with the certainty of a once-faithful dog.

A railway bridge with elaborate Victorian girders, a library with a fine copper dome, some old Georgian townhouse with a plaque commemorating a notorious murder. Locked groomed gardens in the centre of a fine residential square. Soaring spire of a gothic university, soot and time-blackened stone, still floodlit, the shadows of night not yet shaken off. Taken over, as if slotting down into hidden rails, I hasten along avenues and boulevards, remembering some walk… to work perhaps, habitual ritual mind-imprinted over many years, anticipation rising as the jaws of Pavlov's dog. Each vista I turn a corner into, I seem to remember a millisecond before it clogs my eyes. And then at last I glimpse my prize, but not as I thought… the university faculty where perhaps I worked, but something else, more immediate, here in front of me, some urgent memory clothed in murk: a refurbished old hotel, of industrial era brick and clay tiles. This means something important, my heart rate is rising, a blockage in my brain throbbing with a floodtide of meaning dammed up behind it.

I stop and stand in the street in front of its dread façade looming up seven stories above me, and know at last I stand in hell. Cars in the street either side of me are not moving, but neither are they empty. Drivers and passengers are frozen still, eyes and mouths open, halted upon a word and phrase. Gradually I understand this city's peculiar silence and its haze. I step forward and climb the steps, and know and expect the familiar face of the receptionist, remember the colour of her hair and eyes, the cut of her clothes. She too is frozen of course, as are a handful of other guests in poses of movement to and fro across the entrance hall with its chequered marble floor and dusty vaulted ceiling. I move close to each standing guest and run my hand in front of their eyes, check their mouth for breath. And as I rotate around them a peculiar phenomenon unfolds itself: a very fine black line runs down each of their backs from the crown of their heads and across the outside of their clothes, as if they are each simulacrums imperfectly composed. Something Mustafa said about life not being real begins to echo through me, making me feel sick and scared.

I am unprepared for what happens next, as leaning nearer to the black line across the back of a teenage girl's blonde hair, the blackness expands into a growing dot then fills my vision and draws me in. Slurping, sliding of reality, as if stumbling on a fatal riverbank. Her entire body becomes as some masquerading costume I can live and breath within. I look out through her eyes, see the whole view of the reception hall around me, can hear my own blood and heartbeat amplified as if I'm trapped inside an echoing dungeon. I panic and try to scream and by accident more than skill find I am ejected backwards to where I was, outside her again. Shaken, shivering, I move around the large space of the marble hall, circling like a wounded predator or hounded prey, holding my breath, tiptoeing, as if I am about to wake these strange sleepers. Oh that I would. What's worse is somehow knowing that I never could. Here we are, I try another, then another, a middle-aged man, an old woman, I find the spot on the back of their skulls and feel it expand for me and draw me in. Inside each time is a strange silence and suspension, broken only by the din of my own breath. I try to calm myself, and beyond this begin to feel their lives, their memories and intentions, the hurried rivers of their consciousness, frozen in spate, hopeful, despairing, happy or irate. I panic again, too much, this overwhelming knowledge flooding me, I leap back out and back away, closing over my watertight doors, my mental gates.

To the receptionist now, I return my attention and go to stand at her side and her back, and stepping into her mind as if into a cinema hushed in a Saturday matinee, I retrieve her memory, a picture of me taking a key from her, being given a room number, a few minutes before. I go to the lifts, remembering all too well the way, and press the button. Peculiarly, it works, as if machines are immune to this sleeping beauty spell. And yet, if it would only stop and entomb me halfway through its journey that might be more relief than I can tell. Rather than to face what's coming next. But time is an inexorable ocean here. Doors opening, the sixth floor hallway, the carpets, the faded paintings on the wall, all too familiar as if seen only yesterday, but haven't years gone by? Surely? Someone wake me from this childhood nightmare before I cry out, before I... die.

The room is unlocked of course, something I must have thought through once, and there in the middle of the room is... myself. As in a mirror but real, in three dimensions, seated on a chair. I spin around, look at the wardrobe mirrors and am relieved (or am I?) to see myself there standing, two versions, this one I am and the other seated, frozen. Not unreal, not dreaming, but seemingly alive, I strive to make sense of this contrivance. And yet, I'm denying the truth before my eyes even now. The red specks on the carpet, the spray in the air behind him. I rotate around my seated self. No need to look for a way in, for the back of his head is gone, and in his mouth a firing gun.

I know that in a second I will run to the en-suite sink and throw up violently, but for the moment I remain in a spell of ultimate fascination, recognising even the dull metallic sheen of a bullet poised in air, exiting my head and taking with it: fragmented brain matter to splatter, everywhere. Scared? Why should we be, how can we be, when we have ventured beyond such a final revelation? God lets us off with shock it seems when we stumble upon what is above our station to take in. Reality breaks in. No more hinting. Sprinting. My stomach erupts and I am crying out in the toilet, hands upon the porcelain. The universe exploding from its core of primal thoughtless pain, my whole being pouring down the drain. I regain composure at last and wipe my mouth, and looking in the mirror, suddenly jump and turn about. Phew. Nothing's changed. This deranged world is filled with living tailors' dummies, but more terrible than their stasis would be if they were to move again somehow. I need to get away from here, outside this nightmare, to somewhere there is no one to confront me with their frozen deathlike scorn. I am surrounded by the dead it seems, disguised in living form.

I go to the window, part the curtains and am somehow relieved to see that the cars below have not moved, that the zombies are inert and harmless. Then I see them. Even after this, the strangest thing of all, the only moving creatures perhaps in all of Urbis apart from myself: two adult deer, a hind and stag with pure white coat and horns are walking down the street between the cars. And in slow dreamlike motion, inevitable as drowning, they pass the hotel then halt and turns their heads to look up, up at this window and at me. Instinctively, I scrabble for the window hooks and hoist the bottom sash open, thrust my head out into the much-needed fresh air, and call out some crazy wordless cry, forlorn and hollow. They walk on and turn again, more knowingly than any animal ought to, as if to say: follow.

And I do. I must. Running, hurrying, not so much struck with fear now as like a hunter, a man consumed by lust for the most beautiful woman in all creation. The deer are the key. To follow them, to find and touch them, then I might be free... of whatever this is, of whatever foul spell Urbis has done to me. I flee the doomed room with one last glance at the bloodied, halted parody of me. At least it seems I will not rot, no flies and maggots defile my image with their vile machinations. Acceleration. Down the corridors and down the stairs, taking no chances this time of this strange stage set's rules catching me unawares. Out through the echoing marble hall, my footsteps clopping in melancholy thrall to this appalling scenario, absurdity, necessity to follow, calling out in the street after white deer already cantering, moving out of reach.

I run and run, my heart and lungs pumping, seeing the deer wait and turn then gallop down a fresh street, weaving between static buses and cars. The sky above me, the early morning light still seems as frozen as the people. Am I dead? –I ask myself, and if so can I ever tire? And certainly I feel unusually fit and light of foot. Indeed, if dead, I scarcely ever felt this good alive. Diving past the windows of a bus, I glimpse within: arrays of frozen faces and slow for a second in morbid fascination. Those half-dead eyes numbed by dread anticipation of their morning's humiliations and slaveries in return for meagre pay, the dim hope of happiness at the week's end, return into the arms of those who suffer boredom as they do, rocking each other together like crying babes. Then in the reflection in the glass, I see as a reminder the white stag's ghostly form pausing, circling again, drawing me on. We reach a shopping mall and the horned phantom hastens up the steps and lures me in. In early morning light, boosted by insipid electric illumination I run past shoppers clutching bags, a little girl kneeling to pat her dog. Am I dead? –I ask again, and pause to run my fingers through the curls of her hair and that of her dog. Warm and comforting, some kind of foundation stone my mind is reaching out to clutch. Are they still alive but in another time stream? And if so then what am I to them? My strange momentary touch an eerie breeze from nowhere, a blessing from an unseen angel that a lifetime's reflection will never reconcile with rationality? Up ahead, I hear a bellowing, a stomping of hooves, an impatient butting of horns against shop windows. I must away.

Across a bridge now the white hind and stag lead me, and down below in some great gulf I see motorway cars paused and interwoven in a pall of pollution, misery and frustration, suspended in solution. Now trotting down broad stairs, I jump three at a time, trying to catch up, to catch my guides unaware. They turn and face me and the stag lowers his horns and scliffs his hooves, sparking off the granite slabs. Instinctively I recoil against the steps, clutching the handrails. His cold eyes line me up for a second for some fierce trajectory, considering it. Then he throws his head back as if laughing, snorting, and turns and speeds away with his mate in tow, both looking back. It's all been a game, a ruse, to disabuse me of my illusions of any power, powerless before their greater power, his horns, his glower.

The game goes on for hours, across car parks, housing estates, railway lines. The deer lead me past workmen with dust-masks on, feet poised on pneumatic drills, a square full of pigeons being fed by an old bag lady, each bird frozen in a thrilling trill of flight and feathers, I leap up and pluck some flecks of bread out of the air into my mouth. The bread tastes real, reminding me sweetly of the belief that I am still alive. I must hold onto this. If I lag behind, the stag and hind contrive to find me and flush me out. I cross a sport court filled with ladies working out in tight Lycra. The beads of sweat are a glorious eternal glow upon their foreheads. The frozen eyes like those of china dolls, fixed on thoughts of their day ahead, I slip behind one, looking for the black line and try to hide within her head. Inside it's nice but soon I hear the stag's bellows and jabbing at my heels. I who thought I was the follower am now the put-upon and hounded, the betrayed.

At last, noticing some tiredness in my limbs, we approach the northern outskirts of Urbis. I grab a roll and a can of juice from a street vendor's stall, and laugh aloud to think I could have taken anything I'd wanted in this city for free. I take some coins from a frozen passer-by's pocket and toss them behind me in payment, a joke only for me. The deer wait at the street's end, heads bowed, frowning, disregarding of my clowning. The endless domain of tarmac is breaking up, and again I begin to see more forest. Strange wastelands of abandoned warehouses, reclaimed by regiments of trees. I see them differently now, from this weird perspective of halted time. The trees are ransacking man's work, just as violently and methodically as man thinks he's fighting back and controlling the wilderness. Except the trees are slower and stronger and more ancient, and will win. It is all a battle, grander and more exquisite than I ever could have seen, and there in front bound my heralds, ice white, supremely beautiful and clean, horns and hoofs brashly trashing branches and fences in their stride like pulling curtains, tearing veils aside, sniffing out the lost places where secret truths may hide.

We reach the boundary at last where Urbis runs out and Suburbia begins. Suddenly the weather lifts and shifts, weak haze turns to early summer morning light, scintillating bright. I hear birds begin to sing, as if some button has been pressed, the pause released, and now here's the thing: Up ahead, as the deer both go through this elusive border, I see their colour wash from white to reddish brown. They trot a little more, then stop and turn around, watching me as if proud of this little trick. I feel some change come over me also, and look down at my chest and hands, but can find nothing tangible, only a feeling of joy as the clouds depart and the morning light expands. We have escaped the urban sprawl and reached green fields and moorlands.

My deer skip ahead and a new lightness fills my steps. I recognise this place, the outskirts of Suburbia where I started out my journey what seems now like oh so long ago. Soon I will reach the little town square and ask directions, give out a name, look for the girl named Thea and hope that my brother's last words were not said in evil or in jest. Pray that she remembers me with such fervour as I her. Would that be too much to aspire to? On this summer's morn, with all of Nature rising up in joy around me, birds and flies making busy haste, the scent of effulgent life bursting forth in flower and frond, it does not seem beyond the scope of hope that I might find her face again. Her grace, her tenderness that lets my spirit finds its calm at last.

Blast. I should have known fate would have a wicked card or two still shimmied up her sleeve. I can't believe my eyes. Quelle cruel surprise. A van comes racing over the hill, the stag pauses on the tarmac, takes one last look back towards me, and is killed. Horrid sound of abrupt collision of bone and metal. I even hear the driver swearing from his open window, slowing only for a second, concerned for his beloved bodywork. His handiwork is done, Nature's miracle unworked in a second of ignorance. My blood boils in my veins, I cry out and run forward, leaping over clumps of bracken. When I get there the road is quiet, the culprit long gone over the next rise. I kneel and touch the warm furred flesh, smell the red leaking blood. My guide was just a deer it seems, no more or less an angel or a miracle than any other, and yet truly: that is miracle enough. My eyes fill with tears.

My head clears and I stand up, backing away in recognition. I know this moment from before. I have come to some crossroads. I am expected to hoist the bleeding deer onto my shoulders and carry it down into the town centre of Suburbia. Expected? Who watches me here? As if in answer, I hear a rustle from the bracken and branches and glimpse a pale figure in a thicket nearby hurrying away. The hind bereaved, torn but resolved to leave her mate behind? I cry out and move about, trying to get a decent view, a better angle through all the tangle. I refute fate's repetition. I will not hoist the bleeding carcass, but find out who observes me. I run along the road then see her at a turn in the woods: a woman in a long white dress has left the thicket and is hurrying across an open field, looking back occasionally in fear, hoisting the lower reaches of her cotton above the rotten mud. I have not forgotten. Her head is a glowing blonde or red. No, it is a light, no face at all. The lady Elissa moving ever further away, getting smaller. Just like the deer, does she mean for me to follow? And then in a strange moment she turns one last time before vanishing over the hillside, beyond which I know Suburbia nestles, and seems to whisper this phrase straight into my head (or perhaps it is but the wind among the nettles): *Desire Is A Mirage.*

Is she an oracle, a sphinx, a witch, a mage? What are we to make of such an aphorism? And yet, gazing upon the fond curves and lines of the backlands of Suburbia, the stage set of superimposed planes of hedgerowed fields and moors, I find the answer is there filling my eyes: horizons, and all that they comprise, have led me on through all of life's great enterprise. We travellers are but stooges tossed upon the twisting back of Nature, a great she-serpent who lures and then awaits us, always contriving lest we become complacent with her fleeting prizes, to replace one race instantaneously with another goal, another face. You feel malcontent as you grow older with these deceptions? Have faith, her embrace in death is no disappointment, but more warm and more of an anointment than all the tawdry treasures of earthly wealth. She loves you as only a true mother can, modestly, misunderstood and unrequited, and with stealth. Her immortal gift is not the laughable po-faced sham paraded by religions, but being born again continually, recycled and resplendent in all your atoms.

And so, at last, I am laughing. Alive in the sunlight and not daunted or worried by life's strange riddles and repetitions. I break the pattern, I do as I please, free will is sweet. Leaving the road, and skirting the trees, I cross the field towards where last I saw Elissa. And in time I arrive at the top of the wooded ridge and look down into the valley beyond. Suburbia lies there, tranquil, familiar and fond. But now among the trees to my left I notice something new, which if I knew of once, its memory has long gone and this reacquaintance feels fresh as a breath of wind. A ruined tower, medieval at least, its ramparts interwoven with branches and bowers as if wrestling slowly with an ancient beast. Again, that déjà vu, the feeling that this picture has been renewed many times in many lives. I turn back to the horizon and there it is, the memory explained. That sea out there was once much further in. I dreamt of this in a ruined house in Sylvia, connected to that odd machine. It was the life of a seer many centuries ago. That tower was not so tumbled and jumbled then, but a well-built thing whose walls I walked and dwelt within. I venture closer and find a plaque of explanation, faded somewhat, but lovingly engraved, by the National Trust for the erudition of dog-walkers and jogger-stalkers:

The Ruins of the Tower of Erceldoune

Legend records that this site was once the palace of one Laird Thomas Learmonth, known to history as "True Thomas" and "Thomas The Rhymer". He was said to have had the power of prophecy, gifted to him by the Queen of the faeries, who he met and kissed one day whilst out alone in the woods, and spent seven years with in her kingdom underground before returning to this world as if no time had passed. Thomas was said to have predicted the death of King Alexander the Third, the battle of Bannockburn and the union of Scotland and England under a king born of a French queen. He predicted that London will one day sink beneath the sea. Later in life, a servant came to tell him that a mysterious snow white hart and hind had been seen, walking along the streets of the village outside his tower. Thomas knew this to be a sign that the queen of Elfland was calling in her side of the bargain at last, in return for the powers she had gifted him. He quietly left the castle and followed the deer out of the town and was never seen or heard of again.

So. That makes me feel gey queer. I best be getting out of here. No sign of Elissa, or is that a flickering white light down there I see, twinkling for a moment, or just the windshield of a car in summer's heat? I recognise her lighthouse, ornate glass palace on the distant outskirts of town, perhaps I see a door closing there as she withdraws herself, her trail of breadcrumbs having brought me home at last, my heart aghast. Her work is done. But my business lies elsewhere. Time for my feet to take me roving, scrambling, winding down, towards the edges of the well-appointed back gardens of privileged Suburbia, where happy complacency reclines intent on mowing and pruning neat-away each scowl and frown. Why fight it, just because we know in our guilt-ridden hearts that in night time on some other side of the planet or indeed the city, someone else is knifed or drug-addicted or suicidally drowned every minute? Don't spoil our garden party with your rage, Nadir. Poverty and inequality are old as Carthage, part and parcel of civilisation's thrills and spills. It's just the vanity and ignorance of the privileged that kills. Let them satisfy me that they have seen and wept and understood, and I might consent to pass them by with my bloodied deer, my hoisted rood.

At last, my feet bring me full circle, back into the quaintly cobbled pedestrian precinct of Suburbia. And truth be told, after the cold nightmare of Urbis, I am overwhelmed just to see so many living people moving happily about. Their every breath is joy and celebration, life's music manifest in endless invention, organised and harmonious as Bach, unfolding in mathematical precision across the stars, the confident beauty our planet has birthed. I feel as if I have walked right around the Earth, on these same humble feet, just to bring myself back again, exhausted, to this street. Everything looks the same, or does it? Can we be sure, gone once around the globe, that what we return to is the same? Or does not every journey, through time as through space, necessitate a different view, a different face? The statue of Athena is there, the war memorial, brassy, dipped in blood. But she is goddess of wisdom as well as war. A contradiction only a virgin could contain. I see now the hope she lifts skywards in her cup of flame, is not the glorification of bloodshed, but the hope that blood once spilt has not been so in vain. I stop and kneel. I am humbled. I must begin again.

A mumble at my side. I open my eyes and rouse myself back to everyday life, the Saturday crowds swirling past in tides. I am looking at a face I know. It is Weasel, grown older now, more grey and bent, the light within his playful eyes somewhat dim, but still brimming enough with mischief for me not to doubt it's him. I stand and we embrace without reserve. *Weasel, my dear friend. I am so sorry that I left. I thought it was you I hurt, when in fact I left myself bereft. Why do we not understand friendship until we forsake it and it us? Why do we miss that it itself is all, the prime ingredient even in what we call true love when the tide of age has swept all the dross away?*

Zenith, he says, *it is splendid to see you in these parts again. But you best be careful. Do you not see the scowls and scolding looks from all these passers-by, who recognise you from their televisions and Sunday papers? Zenith the racketeer, extortionist, drug-smuggler and rapist?*

What?! I am stunned. *What name did you just call me by?*

Shhh! Don't make me shout it louder. Did you not see that fellow passing there? Doctor Tolleson...remember him? I'm quite sure he identified you well enough, but chose to play all anonymous and gruff, averting eyes for fear of being recognised as once your confidante. Zenith, times like these you find out who your real friends are. Invariably ne'er do wells and losers with nothing more to lose like me, scarred and discarded, ancient and patient as trees. The likes of us, hit rock bottom, with nothing to lose, can do just as we please.

I gaze after Doctor Tolleson, older and greyer too as it happens, but something odd occurs to my eyes that makes me shake my head in disbelief, as if struggling to dispel an optical illusion caused by some contusion. He looks so like... another doctor... Stockbridge, and come to think about it, even Weasel, he looks... no, it makes no sense. Confusion for a moment, then I regain my composure, cover up my exposure, remember my mission and my most urgent disclosure. *Weasel, I've come back here to find a girl I met in Oceania, who I'm told has found her way here. It is a small enough place and I recall you always had your ear so near the ground that folk were apt to stand on your head and crack it like a chestnut. Thea is her name, an unusual enough refrain and appellation for these parts. Is such knowledge outwith or within your crazed domain?*

Follow me, Zenith, he says, wrapping his cloak around him and rolling his eyes around his shoulders like a penitent hoisting boulders, dramatic spy and thief in his own warped beliefs, taking me away from the now faintly-menacing crowds with a sense of palpable relief. Somewhere in the background I glimpse an antiquated bicycle creaking across the precinct, leaking oil like a dream of a memory of someone called Mary, limping up and down like a steampunk penny farthing, painful to watch and startling the starlings. Through many leafy lanes and avenues Weasel leads me past the hum of bees in hedgerows and the gently-heard clickings of tennis balls on secluded lawns and ice in jugs of orange squash on silver trays. Oh Suburbia has changed so blissfully-little as ever, since I've been away! Until at last we part again on a quiet doorstep, promising to meet up again that evening and strike up the old tunes together as of old, providing music in the pubs for the despairing and the cold, rekindling the warmth and romance of life's dance in limbs grown loath and weary. *Your face we might have to disguise, mind...* he says, *with a false moustache or a blind man's glasses. That should help gain the coin and pity of the lassies.*

Alone then, I ring the doorbell and wait. Weight. The tolling of ancient bells as of a church spire lost beneath the sea. Oh please Fate bring back my Aphrodite, Thea, across the waves of all my trials and travails, redeem our suffering as a madman marooned on an island spots white passing sails. The door opens and we both sharply take in our breath. Such recognition is both life and death. Out of sorts and full of tears, she retreats suddenly into the darkness of her home, but significantly I notice when I stop shaking... she has not closed or locked the door. This test, this enigma, is of my own making. I walk tentatively in, and hear her crying, and crying out a name. A husband, her husband? As I enter the living room, I hear footsteps cascading down the stairs, but more light and joyous than any adult. A beautiful child runs to her side and buries his little head among her arms and chest.

The sun is out, the patio doors drawn wide. And there in due course Cynthia and I sit side by side on wicker chairs, each grown older, each grown wise. *Why did you leave me, Nadir? Did you not hear afterwards that I was pregnant with your child? I sent out letters, messengers everywhere. But my husband despised me for the betrayal. Who could fail to understand that, or blame him after all? You ruined me, you brought about my fall. I was thrown out on the streets, reviled by this hypocritical town. I set out to find you, to deceive you, to bring you down. The most successful artist of his generation who had discarded me like a circus clown. And now around us, look at all this devastation, emotional debris, see how love thwarted has brought all the world come crashing down. And then you have the temerity, the incivility, the imbecility, to turn up on my doorstep declaring your undying love. Are you the same person or an impostor seeking to foster my son and rekindle my blighted love? Could two people forgive each other such transgressions? Would such intercession provoke celebration or laugher I wonder, from those who watch above?*

The birds are singing sweetly, the bees going about their business with the confident patience that built Babel and Babylon. Our lives are short and all too soon we will be gone. The child plays at our feet among the geraniums and phormiums, in two voices, one stern and harsh, the other soft and sweet, fighting some imaginary battle or engaged in heated debate, one wishing to give peace and kindness, the other, afraid of rejection, seeking for such weakness to berate. He is two people I see, not yet fully formed or unified, his duality a fluid and dynamic state. *He has his father's eyes...* Cynthia smiles, the first touch of sunlight returning to her eyes.

...And his imaginary friend, I append, understanding finally that in order to begin, I at last, the whole charade of self, must dissolve and end. I reach out my hand and close my eyes, and somewhere out there among the blind heat of summer, as when I was a boy lying in June meadows with my eyes closed and watching the changing patterns behind the lids: I ask and hope that there is love and tenderness up ahead, in the sky or in the world, in the indescribable

excitement of another human being's heart. Let me live and let me play my part. I have always seen the future, that is easy, but not the goal. Only now have I truly seen inside another person's soul. We are here to carry each other, lame and frail, across this darkened land. I feel the touch upon my finger tips at last. She takes my hand.

I am Zarathustra. True Thomas The Rhymer, old timer, social climber. The supple shuttle of the present, master of the warp and weave, the bobbin through which the loom of time speaks, threading and knitting and sewing all past and future into my fabric, my soul. Black as coal and light as long white summer nights. Red hot and melancholy blue. I am Nadir, I am Zenith. And so, dear reader, are you.

~

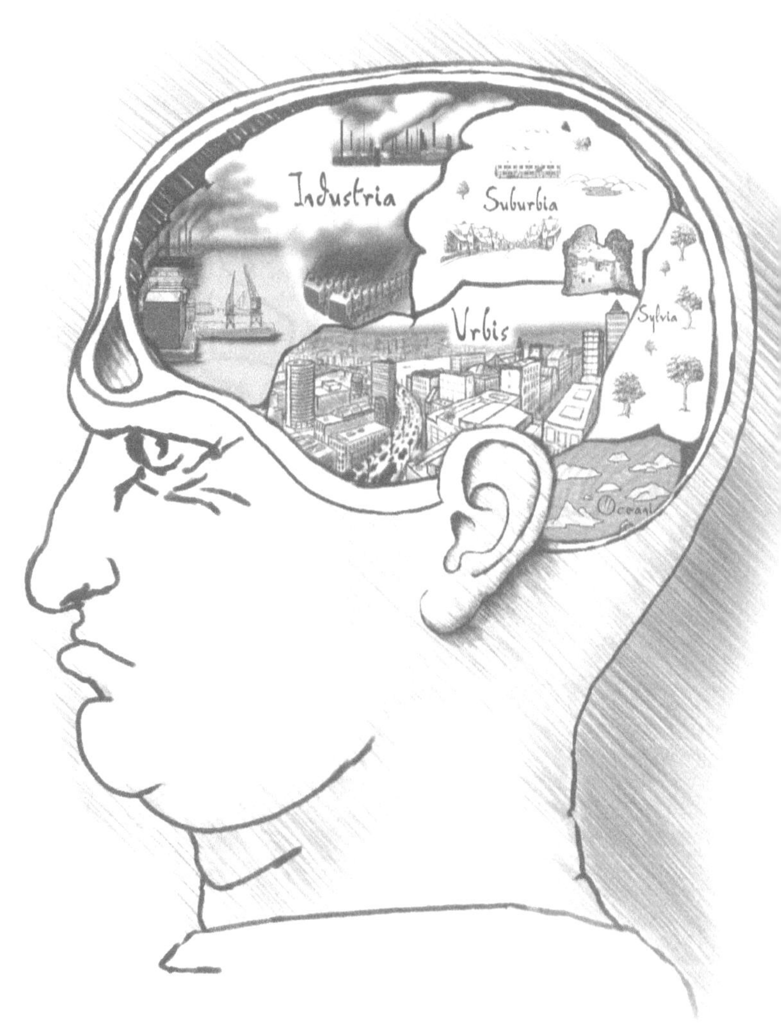

Industria
Suburbia
Urbis
Sylvia
Ocean

Acknowledgements

An alphabetical thank you to all inspirers, encouragers and supporters...

Nina Allan. Allen Ashley. Calum Barnes (for Pynchon). Martin Bax (for Ambit). Alison Buck, Peter et Al at Elsewhen. Terry Grimwood. Andrew Hook. Rachel Kendall (for feedback & input). Robert Leitch (for Flann O'Brien). Linda Jackson (for Rap). Adam Lowe. Jet McDonald. Rona MacDonald. Steve Rapaport (for Lethem). Agnes Rennie. David Rix. Sue Reid Sexton. Jacqueline Smith. Ally Thompson.

...and apologies to all those left out.

Elsewhen Press

an independent publisher specialising in Speculative Fiction

Visit the Elsewhen Press website at elsewhen.press for the latest information on all of our titles, authors and events; to read our blog; find out where to buy our books and ebooks; or to place an order.

Elsewhen Press

an independent publisher specialising in Speculative Fiction

ENTANGLEMENT
DOUGLAS THOMPSON

FINALLY, TRAVEL TO THE STARS IS HERE

In 2180, travel to neighbouring star systems has been mastered thanks to quantum teleportation using the 'entanglement' of sub-atomic matter; astronauts on earth can be duplicated on a remote world once the dupliport chamber has arrived there. In this way a variety of worlds can be explored, but what humanity discovers is both surprising and disturbing, enlightening and shocking. Each alternative to mankind that the astronauts find, sheds light on human shortcomings and potential while offering fresh perspectives of life on Earth. Meanwhile, at home, the lives of the astronauts and those in charge of the missions will never be the same again.

Best described as philosophical science fiction, *Entanglement* explores our assumptions about such constants as death, birth, sex and conflict, as the characters in the story explore distant worlds and the intelligent life that lives there. It is simultaneously a novel and a series of short stories: multiple worlds, each explored in a separate chapter, a separate story; every one another step on mankind's journey outwards to the stars and inwards to our own psyche. Yet the whole is much greater than the sum of the parts; the synergy of the episodes results in an overarching story arc that ultimately tells us more about ourselves than about the rest of the universe.

Douglas Thompson's short stories have appeared in a wide range of magazines and anthologies. He won the Grolsch/Herald Question of Style Award in 1989 and second prize in the Neil Gunn Writing Competition in 2007. His first book, *Ultrameta*, published in 2009, was nominated for the Edge Hill Prize, and shortlisted for the BFS Best Newcomer Award. *Entanglement* is his fifth novel.

ISBN: 9781908168153 (epub, kindle)
ISBN: 9781908168054 (336pp paperback)

Visit bit.ly/EntanglementBook

Elsewhen Press

an independent publisher specialising in Speculative Fiction

The Lost Men
An Allegory
David Colón

In a world where the human population has been decimated, self-reliance is the order of the day. Of necessity, the few remaining people must adapt residual technology as far as possible, with knowledge gleaned from books that were rescued and have been treasured for generations. After a childhood of such training, each person is abandoned by their parents when they reach adulthood, to pursue an essentially solitary existence. For most, the only human contact is their counsel, a mentor who guides them to find 'the one', their life mate as decreed by Fate. Lack of society brings with it a lack of taboo, ensuring that the Fate envisioned by a counsel is enacted unquestioningly. The only threats to this stable, if sparse, existence are the 'lost men', mindless murderers who are also self-sufficient but with no regard for the well-being of others, living outside the confines of counsel and Fate.

Is Fate a real force, or is it totally imagined, an arbitrary convention, a product of mankind's self-destructive tendency? In this allegorical tale, David Colón uses an alternate near-future to explore the boundaries of the human condition and the extent to which we are prepared to surrender our capacity for decisions and self-determination in the face of a very personally directed and apparently benevolent, authoritarianism. Is it our responsibility to rebuke inherited 'wisdom' for the sake of envisioning and manifesting our own will?

David Colón is an Assistant Professor of English at TCU in Fort Worth, Texas, USA. Born and raised in Brooklyn, New York, he received his Ph.D. in English from Stanford University and was a Chancellor's Postdoctoral Fellow in English at the University of California, Berkeley. His writing has appeared in numerous journals, including *Cultural Critique*, *Studies in American Culture*, *DIAGRAM*, *How2*, and *MELUS*. *The Lost Men* is his first book.

ISBN: 9781908168146 (epub, kindle)
ISBN: 9781908168047 (192pp paperback)

Visit lost-men.com

Elsewhen Press

an independent publisher specialising in Speculative Fiction

Bookworm
Christopher Nuttall

Elaine is an orphan girl who has grown up in a world where magical ability brings power. Her limited talent was enough to ensure a magical training but she's very inexperienced and was lucky to get a position working in the Great Library. Now, the Grand Sorcerer – the most powerful magician of them all – is dying, although initially that makes little difference to Elaine; she certainly doesn't have the power to compete for higher status in the Golden City. But all that changes when she triggers a magical trap and ends up with all the knowledge from the Great Library – including forbidden magic that no one is supposed to know – stuffed inside her head. This unwanted gift doesn't give her greater power, but it does give her a better understanding of magic, allowing her to accomplish far more than ever before.

It's also terribly dangerous. If the senior wizards find out what has happened to her, they will almost certainly have her killed. The knowledge locked away in the Great Library was meant to remain permanently sealed and letting it out could mean a repeat of the catastrophic Necromantic Wars of five hundred years earlier. Elaine is forced to struggle with the terrors and temptations represented by her newfound knowledge, all the while trying to stay out of sight of those she fears, embodied by the sinister Inquisitor Dread.

But a darkly powerful figure has been drawing up a plan to take the power of the Grand Sorcerer for himself; and Elaine, unknowingly, is vital to his scheme. Unless she can unlock the mysteries behind her new knowledge, divine the unfolding plan, and discover the truth about her own origins, there is no hope for those she loves, the Golden City or her entire world.

Bookworm was Christopher's second fantasy novel to be published by Elsewhen Press, and won the Gold Award in the Adult Fiction category of the 2013 Wishing Shelf Independent Book Awards.

ISBN: 9781908168320 (epub, kindle)
ISBN: 9781908168221 (368pp, paperback)

Visit bit.ly/Bookworm-Nuttall

Elsewhen Press

an independent publisher specialising in Speculative Fiction

GHOSTS ON THE
PRAIRIES
A SACRED LAND STORY

TANYA REIMER

Some things are worth a fight. Strong words that Antoine's father drilled into him. After his father mysteriously vanishes one night, Antoine must find another income or he risks losing the Sacred Land that his father swore to protect.

On a well-paying ranch, Antoine meets Emma, a victim of underground slavery. Fighting for her freedom costs him his home, his sister, his best friend, and puts in question all of his values. If he succeeds, will she and her son fit into his world?

The prairies of 1916-19 come alive with bootleggers, slavery, fools in sheets, haunting spirits, shifty tunnel runners, and even exploding churches. *Ghosts on the Prairies* is alternative history suspense incorporating the paranormal and infused with romance.

Born and raised in Saskatchewan, Tanya enjoys using the tranquil prairies as a setting to her not-so-peaceful speculative fiction. She is married with two children which means among her accomplishments are the necessary magical abilities to find a lost tooth in a park of sand and whisper away monsters from under the bed.

Tanya was fifteen when she wrote her first column. She has a diploma in Journalism/Short Story Writing. Today, she actively submits to various newspapers, writes and publishes the local Francophone newsletter for her community, and maintains a blog at Life's Like That.

Ghosts on the Prairies, a Sacred Land Story for adults, is her debut novel.

ISBN: 9781908168535 (epub, kindle)
ISBN: 9781908168436 (356pp paperback)

Visit bit.ly/GhostsPrairies

Elsewhen Press
an independent publisher specialising in Speculative Fiction

The Janus Cycle
Tej Turner

The Janus Cycle can best be described as gritty, surreal, urban fantasy. The over-arching story revolves around a nightclub called Janus, which is not merely a location but virtually a character in its own right. On the surface it appears to be a subcultural hub where the strange and disillusioned who feel alienated and oppressed by society escape to be free from convention; but underneath that façade is a surreal space in time where the very foundations of reality are twisted and distorted. But the special unique vibe of Janus is hijacked by a bandwagon of people who choose to conform to alternative lifestyles simply because it has become fashionable to be "different", and this causes many of its original occupants to feel lost and disenchanted. We see the story of Janus unfold through the eyes of seven narrators, each with their own perspective and their own personal journey. A story in which the nightclub itself goes on a journey. But throughout, one character, a strange girl, briefly appears and reappears warning the narrators that their individual journeys are going to collide in a cataclysmic event. Is she just another one of the nightclub's denizens, a cynical mischief-maker out to create havoc or a time-traveller trying to prevent an impending disaster?

Tej Turner is fresh out of University, where he partied vigorously and studied Creative Writing and Ancient History to sharpen his craft. He has just begun branching out as a writer and been published in anthologies, including *Impossible Spaces* (Hic Dragones) and *The Bestiarum Vocabulum* (Western Legends Press). When he is not gallivanting around the world trekking jungles and exploring temples, reefs, and caves he is usually based in Cardiff, where he works by day, writes by moonlight, and squeezes in the occasional trip to roam around megalithic sites and the British countryside. The next time he has enough money he will be flying off on another adventure.

The Janus Cycle is his first published novel. He is currently engaged in writing an epic fantasy trilogy.

ISBN: 9781908168566 (epub, kindle)
ISBN: 9781908168467 (224pp paperback)

Visit bit.ly/JanusCycle

About the author

Douglas Thompson's short stories have appeared in a wide range of magazines and anthologies, most recently *Albedo One*, *Ambit*, *Postscripts*, and *New Writing Scotland*. He won the Grolsch/Herald Question of Style Award in 1989 and second prize in the Neil Gunn Writing Competition in 2007. His first book, *Ultrameta*, was published in August 2009, nominated for the Edge Hill Prize, and shortlisted for the BFS Best Newcomer Award, and since then he has published four subsequent novels, *Sylvow* (2010), *Apoidea* (2011), *Mechagnosis* (2012), *Entanglement* (2012) and has two forthcoming in 2014, *The Brahan Seer* and *Volwys*. *The Rhymer* is his eighth novel and the second to be published by Elsewhen Press.

www.ingramcontent.com/pod-product-compliance
Lightning Source LLC
Chambersburg PA
CBHW031958180726
48283CB00008B/2478